# THE COLOR
# OF THE SNOW

# Rüdiger Kremer

# THE COLOR OF THE SNOW

Translated by Breon Mitchell

A New Directions Book

Acknowledgment: Section 18 of *The Color of the Snow* originally appeared in
a slightly different form in *New Directions in Prose and Poetry 41*.
Manufactured in the United States of America
New Directions Books are printed on acid-free paper
First published clothbound and as New Directions Paperbook 743 in 1992
Published simultaneously in Canada by Penguin Books Canada Limited
Library of Congress Cataloging-in-Publication Data
Kremer, Rüdiger, 1942–
[Moij und andere Geschichten um Jakob. English]
The color of the snow / Rüdiger Kremer ; translated by Breon Mitchell.
p.  cm — (New Directions paperbook ; 743)
Translation of : Das Moij und andere Geschichten um Jakob.
ISBN 0–8112–1200–9 : $19.95. — ISBN 0–8112–1208–4 (paperbook) : $9.95
I. Title.
PT2671.R445M6513   1992
833′.914—dc20                                                   91–44000
                                                                  CIP

New Directions books are published for James Laughlin
by New Directions Publishing Corporation,
80 Eighth Avenue, New York 10011

# THE COLOR
# OF THE SNOW

After wondering for some time whether my tale was worth telling, and whether it could be told as it happened, I've decided to write it down according to my own and others' memories and notes, the only way it could have been.

J. L. B.

# I.

Scarcely an hour's walk from the village where I grew up, the little river along which the towns of our valley lie has cut deeply into the yellow-gray sandstone peculiar to the richly-carved churches and public buildings of this region, creating a precipitous ravine so narrow and deep that the sun reaches its bottom only at the height of summer afternoons.

There are many tales about this inaccessible spot—stories of child murderers, crying by night for their drowned children, of innocent hanged men, raging for revenge in storm and wind, of suicides whose incorruptible bodies are torn from their gravel graves by the flooding waters, then buried beneath the deeper eddies—recounted and expanded upon by village elders who vouch for their truth and veracity in an attempt to dissuade the terrified children from drawing too near to its dangerous depths. Yet such stories lure more than they frighten, tempting the wanderer to leave the path that follows the rim of the ravine and clamber down into the uncanny chasm, at the base of which a true mystery remains unsolved to this very day.

Upon a steep and rocky island in the middle of the rushing stream, half-buried by rockslides, so that it is scarcely possible to tell the broken masonry from the fallen stone, stand the remnants of a peculiar dwelling, half cave, half tower, without entrance or windows, traces of a strange and distant life which have withstood even the raging waters of the melting snow.

It's true that this spot may be clearly observed from a safe lookout point on the rim, when the ravine is not shrouded in mist and clouds of spray, but the mystery surrounding these ruins and their builder has continued to lure first the local inhabitants and then even visitors from distant towns to approach them more closely, even though signs have been posted warning people not to leave the paths or overlooks, along with half-a-dozen wooden crosses bearing the names, dates, and oval pictures of mostly very young men who tried to reach the little island and paid for it with their lives.

All sorts of iron devices have been driven into the overhanging cliffs—hooks and rings for ropes, pitons and pegs as steps—and handholds have been cut into the face of the stone as if to mark the way. With the help of these abandoned aids, but by no means without risk, since many of the iron pegs have loosened over time, while others, exposed to the constant spray of the torrent, have totally rusted through, and the handholds in the stone are crumbling away, one may now reach the bottom of the ravine. There is no way, however, to cross the rushing water to the island, not even in the dry season, when the broad gravel bed of the river is totally exposed in the lower part of the valley.

Trapped between the stream and the cliff wall, little more is visible than can be seen from the safety of the heights. The house appears smaller now, scarcely more than four paces square. One can see the artful way in which stones the size of a child's head have been arranged to form the meter-thick walls, the start of a flight of steps leading to a rocky plateau washed bare, small boulders piled into a sort of bulwark, although a tangle of driftwood caught among the stones prevents, even from this distance, any precise sense of the nature of this strange architecture.

If the island could be reached, one might find traces, testimony, scratches on the stone, if nothing else the initials of the man who built a citadel here for a life of evident despair, visible to all, accessible to none.

## 2.

The name they gave the boy they had all been hoping for, born on a late Maundy Thursday morning in forty-four so quickly and smoothly that there wasn't even time to move the mother from the kitchen into the sitting room when, with a small cry, she collapsed onto the brown and yellow flagstone floor before the stove, where the grandmother stout-heartedly cut the umbilical cord and washed him off with the hot water in which they had been steeping onion peels to color the eggs for Easter, was not Trygve, which the mother preferred at first because that was the name of her favorite author; nor Roland, as the father had requested in his long letters from the front, the last of which arrived weeks after he died near Odessa, now tied in bundles by year with blue ribbon and kept in the middle drawer of the old cherry cupboard never to be read again; nor Friederich, after the father fallen in battle, as the grandmother, in proud mourning for her only son, had stubbornly insisted; but, because they saw that the child had been born with a big head and strange eyes, and since they all came to realize, even the mother at last, that the drooling baby, constantly gurgling but never crying, accepted with reluctance at its mother's breast, was weak in the head and showed no signs of ever getting better, as the doctor from the neighboring village confirmed, they named him Jakob, Jakob after his childish old grandfather, who, kept halfway sober for once, carried the bubble-blowing child on a bright sunshiney afternoon a fortnight after Whitsunday on a lace-covered pillow down the main street of the village to be baptized, with tears of joy in his eyes.

Convinced that without divine protection a man would inevitably lose his way in this life, the priest entrusted the boy to the patron saint of the local church and at a signal from the suddenly sobbing grandfather, before anyone could stop him, baptized Jakob Lorenz with a third handful of water and added the name Barthel, in memory of the grandfather's older brother, who, in a fit of unrequited love, had hanged himself from the rafters in the hayloft of the barn.

Old Jakob—who years ago, before he started drinking, had been quite different, a prudent farmer and a passionate hunter who not only provided for his own domestic needs, but also started a business selling surplus crops, achieving a level of prosperity unusual in this poor region—was feared for his sudden temper, which erupted whenever anyone tried to keep him from drinking, or expressed itself in savage curses and murderous threats against anyone in sight whenever he had problems completing some small domestic task because his hands shook for no apparent reason; so everyone was surprised to find that once he was given charge of the barely-weaned child, whenever the others were busy in the house, courtyard, gardens, and fields, he never lost his temper again; indeed, he took little Jakob under his wing with a tenderness no one had ever witnessed before, so that with the exception of the bad habit the old man had of occasionally dipping his finger in whiskey and letting the child suck greedily at it, which in the end was simply laughed at, there seemed no reason to disturb the obvious harmony of the two Jakobs.

Thus the child was gradually given over entirely to the care of the family patriarch, who didn't let him out of his sight, taking him along everywhere, including his secret drinking spots, for even though they no longer kept him from the bottle, he hid his whiskey in the furthest corners of the barn and stalls, a habit he maintained out of distrust even after they began drawing his daily portion from the cask in the locked cellar and setting it in an earthenware jug beside the overturned milk pail he sat on both winters and summers beneath the arched gateway to the barns in his green heavily-patched woolen jacket, hunched over finger-thick hazelnut sticks from the previous year, carving long notches with his hunting knife, talking to himself in a sing-song language which, issuing from his toothless mouth through his grayish-yellow beard as a barely-audible murmur, was understood by no one but little Jakob, who seemed to listen eagerly to the long, pleasant-sounding murmur of the stories as he lay in his basket at the old man's feet, and later, when he could crawl, content and self-absorbed, tied by his left ankle to the middle post of the gate with a calf rope, sitting on the horse-blanket spread in summer upon the cobblestones of the courtyard beneath the linden trees, or in winter upon a layer of straw in the barn, he played with the carefully-carved sticks with their rounded ends, soft as the tips of fingers.

And so little Jakob learned to speak by memorizing the recurring sentences, first joining in on the final words of each story, which ran something like *"Baiff sibbe ailehünne / heisch oibe / aisch ünne,"* then eventually learning to repeat each of the stories in the same sing-song tone, word for word, to the chuckling amazement of those who listened to him in secret behind half-opened doors and windows, for he responded to all requests or commands to demonstrate his strange talent with a stubborn silence.

On a warm October afternoon old Jakob died of a stroke. Over the next few days, without a sign of illness, little five-year old Jakob tried to die like his grandfather, and when he couldn't manage to, he said, with a smile, and so clearly that everyone could understand him: "I'm Moy, that's who I am, Moy."

# 3.

We found the young soldier in March, when the woods above the ravine were still filled with snow.

He lay hidden beneath a bushy pine tree, half-covered with crusted snow, seemingly asleep; his head was leaning against the trunk of the tree, his eyes closed, his hands thrust under his armpits, his feet wrapped in rags, his legs spread wide and stretched out before him. We talked to him, shook him, wiped the crystallized snow from his eyes, and when, straining to lift him, we discovered that he was frozen solid to the ground, we confronted our first dead man, one I recognized immediately by his black hair, when we had removed his hat, as my father. But since the Brigittes explained that he was too young to be anyone's father, we took him for one of the seven lost brothers, come back from America to die in his native land, and called him Jonathan.

We built a brushwood hut to protect him from the snow and promised to visit him every day, to bring him everything he needed as long as he was unable to stand. We brought him a blanket, a woolen shawl, bread, and milk, but it wasn't until a thaw arrived that we were able to bed him down more comfortably and feed him pre-chewed pulp, since he wouldn't take a bite from our bread, or drink from our outstretched hands.

When it got warmer we pulled him out into the sun from his hiding place among the pines, took off his saturated woolen coat to let it dry, and discovered, scarcely a handbreadth away from the small colored band he wore in the buttonhole of his uniform jacket, a deep wound; we cautiously placed our fingers in it, convinced that he would awaken at this touch with a little cry, his eyes filled with wonder as if he were emerging from a hundred-year sleep. But he did not open his eyes, nor lift his head, nor reach out for help, nor awaken, nor did he even bleed from the wound, but instead remained as he was, as senselessly silent and dead as ever, no matter what we said.

Yet as the days turned warmer our dead man seemed to be getting better. His narrow face filled out, his lips relaxed over his teeth, his stomach started to bulge, and finally he began making noises, a soft breath at first, a cough, and then a blubbering moan. Early one morning, when he was finally beginning to smile at the songs the Brigittes were singing, foresters found him and carried him into the village, wrapped in our horse-blanket.

Jonathan was buried by the cemetery wall as an unknown soldier. Even though they hit me several times, I denied knowing him, nor did I betray the Sisters.

# 4.

Enveloped in a long coat crudely stitched together from woolen blankets, the father returned home from the war at noon one warm spring day, opened the kitchen door without knocking, and stood silently for a moment, regarding those eating, who, looking up from their plates one after the other, at first took the man they thought dead for one of the wandering beggars who came along the road each day, alone or in groups, threatening the safety of house and home, so little did the small figure standing in the door resemble the young soldier in a black uniform who had departed seven years ago with the promise to return from the campaign as a victor or not at all; now, when a thick-set man he didn't know sprang up from the head of the table and raised his hand with a curse to order him from the house, whistling for the dog, he revealed who he was; he fended off all embraces, would not eat the green bean soup on the table, nor drink the milk, refused blackberry wine, whiskey, just wanted to sleep, not in the bedroom, which they quickly offered to prepare for him, but in the stable with the cows; he slept wrapped in his rough coat for two days and two nights in an empty calf-stall on chopped oat straw, watched at a loss by his family, who tried to read from his whispering lips what he murmured to himself in his uneasy and fitful sleep.

In the early morning of the third day he was awakened by the grandfather, who poked him gently with his carved cane of knotty pine and, as he sprang up in fright, not realizing for a moment where he was, and tried to duck quickly through the half-open stable door, blocked his way with the words that this child—he pointed to a boy approximately five years of age he was carrying in his arms, in whose broad face the father could recognize, in spite of the strangely-shaped eyes, the features of the man who had greeted him so angrily at the door—had recognized him immediately and knew who he was; he then spoke in a strange sing-song with the child who finally stretched out his arms toward the father, let himself be hugged without a trace of shyness, and after picking the husks and awns from his beard with nimble fingers, kissed him with wet lips on the mouth, spraying him as he spoke strange words the old man translated as an invitation to the morning meal.

The grandfather and the boy took the father by the hand and led him into the kitchen, where the family stood about the laid table. He was urged with a friendly wave to the place at the head of the table, set with the best china and decorated with a bouquet of snowdrops. Before he had even seated himself, coffee was being poured, a basket with thick slices of freshly-baked bread was passed, butter and milk were offered, eggs, cheese and sausages, several kinds of marmalade, syrup, and a pack of foreign cigarettes. But except for the brief phrases normal at a meal, no one said a word for a long time. Only the grandfather and the child whispered quietly to one another in their own language, ignoring the mother's admonishing looks.

Finally, during a quiet moment, the mother reported that they had discussed everything while the father had been sleeping off his exhaustion, and they were all agreed on what to do now that, raised from the dead so to speak, he had returned to his home and his accustomed place. The father interrupted her with a brusque movement of his bullet-riddled hand, asked the man with the coarse face who, still chewing on a piece of buttered toast, had risen to leave the room, to sit back down, and talked about his future. He didn't want to hear or say anything about what had happened during the intervening years. He wanted things to stay just as they were, as if he'd never returned, didn't want to hear any talk about accustomed places, since there weren't any, forbade cancellation of his death certificate, resisted any avowals or assurances, rejected all plans. He asked for a hot bath, clean clothes, for his strange coat to be cleaned and mended, that he be allowed to live in the stableboy's room, and given one hot meal a day. Then, since he was suddenly overcome by a trembling that began in his crippled left hand, and which although he grasped the hand firmly in his sound right, soon spread over his entire body, shocking everyone except for the giggling grandfather and child into silence, he told them about his illness when the effects had at last subsided; he had contracted a fever during forced labor in the swamps as a prisoner of war, which recurred unexpectedly at irregular intervals, but was not communicable; and since he was long accustomed to living with this sickness, he needed neither assistance nor care, at most a certain forbearance, since the fever made him extremely sensitive to noise, and unfortunately a little intolerant, but only during the attacks themselves.

Then he took his homecoming gifts from a pouch attached to his coat and handed the mother an embossed brass vase made from a mortar shell; the wife a bracelet filed from the copper ring of a hand grenade into a tendril of rosebuds; the grandfather a short-stemmed pipe carved from the hardest stone-pine, with a stem turned from the ulna of a wolf; and the tall man a snuffbox made from the antler of a reindeer and originally intended for the farmhand, who had died in the meantime. He'd brought rings and bracelets for the stableboy and the maid, snakes entwining about a wrist or finger, fashioned from airplane metal; and last of all he gave the child a doll within a doll, carved from birch with woodburned decorations.

The first to express his thanks, holding back his tears, was the tall man, whom the wife introduced as their friend Hermann, then all the others hugged and kissed him, until the father fended them off with a laugh, pointing out that he had lice and knew he must smell bad.

The mother prepared a bath for him in the washroom, undid the sweat-stained paper and cloth bandages wrapped about him, and immediately added them to the fire beneath the kettle in which the water for the second bath began to sing. She pared his toenails and fingernails, washed him with good soap, and trimmed every last hair on his body. She added a nosegay of hay flowers and rosemary to the second bath, dried him, dabbed with tincture of alcohol the minor scratches she'd left while shaving him, in spite of all her care, felt the scars of old injuries, annointed his footsore feet with oil, then handed him clean and freshly-ironed underwear, a pair of trousers that were now too large, and a white wool sweater she'd finished knitting even after they'd received notification of his death, and then kept for him, because she alone had never been convinced that he was really dead. The certainty that he would come home had kept her alive over the years, and now she could die in peace.

The father moved into the farmhand's room above the stable, slept for long periods, entered the main living quarters only for evening meals, spoke little, made only a few small requests now and then, mostly for pencils and paper, never discussed how the farm should be run, even if asked, and when they finally reproached him for refusing to accept responsibility for those entrusted to him, for the house and farm and animals, he answered with unusual and therefore frightening vehemence that he had not come back to worry about animals and people, houses and farms, or fields and meadows. He demanded that from now on his meals be placed at the top of the steps leading to his room and forbade any and all visitors.

Since no one knew what to say to this almost enraged set of instructions, during which the father fell into the local dialect for the first time since he'd returned home—something that only struck them later—he was only rarely seen from that point on; for instance walking barefoot through the dew-moistened grass of the orchard in the early morning hours with measured step, wrapped in his woolen blanket-coat, jerking his crippled hand about as if in response to his own inaudible words, or leaving the farm by way of the barn to wander aimlessly about the fields, accompanied by his dog, whose pressing affection passed without a word or gesture of response. Sometimes at night he could be heard wandering about the house, singing once-forbidden songs beneath his breath or, interrupted by fits of coughing, reciting unknown verses aloud as he paced back and forth in his tiny room. He often cried out angrily for silence when no one was making a sound; yet the din of the cattle at feeding time didn't seem to disturb him at all, nor did the rattle of the milk cans morning and night in the courtyard.

When August arrived in a terrible heat wave, the father was attacked by a high fever. The illness didn't last long. Before the heat wave had broken, the sickness had destroyed him, shaking his body with chills and fits of coughing. Behind a pile of blood-stained handkerchiefs they found a stack of letters, each one addressed in steep block letters to little Jakob, and each bearing the exact date upon which it was to be delivered to the boy as he was growing up. They steamed open the first few mysterious letters, and then, when they discovered that each and every one of them said the same thing, they simply tore open the carefully-sealed envelopes and read the same sentence over and over: You are my only-begotten son, in whom I am well pleased, and therefore I say unto you, take nothing upon yourself, and do not allow yourself to be killed in your thirty-third year in return for the promise of salvation.

## 5.

Even though I sit all day at the window, rising from my chair only occasionally to pace the few steps between the wall with the bed and the wall with the wardrobe, I fall asleep early each evening, often before the children have even returned, for my illness tires me so quickly that even on days when I don't have a fever few hours remain to work on my papers. I fall into a deep and dreamless sleep until a terrible thirst overwhelms me, usually around midnight, and I have to get up for a drink. But since water passes almost straight through my sick body, I'm barely asleep again when the pressure on my bladder, which I try to counteract by shifting my position, finally crossing my feet and drawing my legs up against my water-swollen stomach to gain a few last minutes of relief, initiates a long period of sleeplessness. After I've relieved myself I'm thirsty again; and so it goes, at increasingly shorter intervals which I attempt to lengthen by delaying the rapid satisfaction of these urgently alternating needs, holding out to myself the promise of the greatest possible relief from the most acute pangs, until, sitting on the toilet, I drink to the point of bursting, and feel within myself the cold column of water from the top of my throat to the end of my urinary tract.

I would not adopt these methods—for I could instead suck stones as the Indians do to stimulate their salivary glands to greater secretion during their long desert wanderings, or, with less risk, since the stones, sucked smooth, are easily swallowed by accident or in sleep, I could place a damp cloth over my mouth and suck out the moisture drop by drop—were it not for the wealth of words and images that the coldness of the inner column of water brings with it night after night, continuing to spin out for me the long story of the three unhappy, equally-sensitive Brigittes who, from the night I first invented them to overcome my insomnia, refuse to quit my mind.

Only yesterday the youngest Brigitte was captured and delivered defenseless to the savage desires of dark pirates, but today the other Sisters are sailing toward them with a crew of men ready for anything.

# 6.

Children are kept away when animals are being butchered because butchering frightens children, it makes them cry and mumble incoherently in their sleep. Because you never spoke, nor cried, and never seemed afraid of anything, they let you watch them slaughter the horse.

Some women found the horse while gathering wood, abandoned no doubt by the soldiers as they rapidly withdrew from the area, found it grazing in the woods, and brought it into the village that night with muffled hooves. The men held a counsel and finally decided to slaughter the horse, although it was a punishable offense, and to distribute the meat among the families in the village, so that everyone would be involved and equally culpable. But since none of them had ever slaughtered a horse—calves, yes, and pigs, but not an animal of that size—they had to hire a butcher from a nearby village. He came in the early morning with his tools, looked the animal over, thought it was really too bad to have to slaughter it, named his price, which the men finally agreed to although they found it too high, ate breakfast, chose two men to help him, and set to work.

You were sitting on the sill of the barricaded barn door beside your grandfather, who explained everything to you quietly in your own language. The horse, which the butcher led into the barn on a rope, was a Belgian gelding, brown with a blond mane, a blond tail, and blond tufts at his hooves, at least a half ton, a godsend for any plow, even in the hardest ground. "God, what times these are," your grandfather said, and you repeated, "God, what times these are." The butcher looped the horse's halter through an iron ring in the wall, leaned under the heavy body, speaking to him softly and gently, and passed two chains, attached to pullies anchored high in the rafters for hoisting bales into the hayloft, around his rear fetlocks.

Then the butcher unhitched the horse from the ring in the wall, told his two helpers to hold tight to the halter on each side of the horse's head, took his stun-gun, cocked it, placed it against the forehead of the now nervously snorting horse, and, as the animal jerked its head, said, "Hold tight, I said!" and pulled the trigger. The animal collapsed, fell to the brick floor of the barn with a deafening crash, kicked out one last time with a clatter of chains, shuddered, stretched out its head, and lay still. Do you remember? One of the helpers, who had thrust two fingers through the metal ring on the halter to hold the horse's head, couldn't pull them out in time when the horse collapsed and had the middle finger of his right hand wrenched off, which both you and your grandfather were of one mind in thinking he deserved. And while the men were leading the helper, screaming about his finger, into the house to be cared for by the women, you observed the dead animal and as you'd never seen a dead animal before in your life, it seemed more beautiful and powerful in death than it had in life. "All things," your grandfather said, after making sure that no one else was listening, entrusting you with the secret of life, "All things consist of an inside and an outside. When you take away the outside, you see the inside, and when you take away the inside, you see the soul." Before you could ask about its shape, the men returned, laboriously cranked the horse's carcass up by the rafter chains, severed the jugular vein, caught the streaming blood in a zinc tub, placed ladders against the dangling animal, flayed it with rapid slices, hacked off its head, opened the shimmering red, pink, and blue stomach lining, cut out the entrails, sorted them according to the butcher's instructions into piles of edible parts and offal, threw the man-sized heart back and forth to each other with howls of laughter, looked for and found the bladder during this brief, merry break, punctured it, emptied it into the drain in the floor, and blew it up for you to play with; but since the ball was thrown to you in the barn door, you weren't there to catch it. You were squatting in the middle of the steaming pile of entrails, smeared with blood and excrement, trying your best to untangle the knots and put everything in order, as if you were looking for something. The men picked you up, dragged you from the barn, ignoring both the pleas they'd never heard from you before and your fearsome fits of biting, and when you proved immune to threats and wouldn't settle down, they locked you in the attic.

You stood at the attic window until darkness fell, never taking your eyes from the one open dormer window of the barn so that you wouldn't miss the sight of something white, as small as a handkerchief or as large as a sheet, floating up toward the heavens.

# 7.

The young glazier did not choose his trade, as one might have assumed after the fact, by inclination. Instead he had been guided into it by his father, who wished him to carry on the long-established glass business in the southern city, a shop known for its skillful handmade artifacts, even though glass-making had long since ceased to be regarded as an art. At first he seemed totally unsuited for it since as a child he broke everything he touched, not out of spite, as his father suspected, but from an apparently innate yet totally atypical awkwardness, from which he was carefully weaned by punishments measured according to the value of the object broken, so that later, while still in primary school, when sent to help his father in the workshop, he handled all his assigned tasks with the utmost care. Having thus been raised into a predetermined trade, the thought of another, more pleasing occupation never occurred to him, and only on rare occasions did he envy his two younger brothers, one a judge in the capital, the other a munitions expert in Arabia, who had the good fortune of choosing their paths in life freely due to their position as younger siblings; not so much because he would have preferred to be a judge or munitions expert rather than a glazier, but because he would have liked the chance to live in those distant places. When his father died, and the young glazier could finally run the business the way he wanted to, he began to cut back on the number of windows he installed, or the bedrooms and living rooms he decorated with mirrored ceilings and walls, claiming that he was ill, or too busy, or having difficulty getting materials, until at last, except for small jobs like repairing broken windows after storms, no one asked him to do anything anymore.

Now he traveled through the countryside in his truck loaded with mirrors, kept to isolated country roads, to forest lanes, and to the narrow back alleys of the city, and could not feast his eyes enough on the images his angled mirrors provided of a world gone out of joint. In the evening, when darkness fell, he liked most of all to sit at the edge of the busiest square in the city, on a café terrace, and observe himself in his mirrors among the many brightly-lit windows, imagining the women who cast their shadows on the curtains, beautiful.

# 8.

If someone were to ask me how I'm doing now, through the locked door, I'd say just one sentence to him: since you want to know how I'm doing, I'll say just one sentence to you. I'm feeling fine.

But I'm not feeling fine, and I don't even want to feel fine. Otherwise I'd sit sleeping or dozing in my easy chair. Everyone in the house knows that I spend my less painful days dozing and sleeping in my easy chair. The chair is placed opposite the door, in front of the window that looks out onto the garden. So I could be seen through the keyhole, and still could now, if I hadn't plugged the keyhole with chewed-up paper yesterday, when I had another attack.

Attacks of pain keep a person alert and sharpen perceptions. For example you're not aware of the astonishing amount of saliva produced during the course of a day until you have to swallow it through an inflamed and swollen throat before and after every cough. I swallow, cough, and swallow. I cough softly, covering my mouth with my hand, because I know that a suppressed cough is more annoying than a loud, choking fit of coughing. Whoever is holding his breath to listen at my door hears a tortured rasping, a stifled rattle, a panting struggle for breath, and then the painful sounds of swallowing.

I can tell that the person listening outside is running out of breath, has almost no oxygen left, I can hear the whistling inward gasp he has to take through his open mouth, how he pulls in too much, air his lungs can't hold and keep, which he has to expel loudly and audibly.

I laugh silently, whistle a Chopin waltz through my teeth in airy half-tones and pace barefoot in three-four time back and forth through the darkened room, using every loosely-nailed floor board I can find to creak beneath my foot.

By dint of long practice I can hold my breath longer than anyone else. I can measure precisely how much air my listeners have left by means of my own steady, diaphramatic breathing. And just before they run out of breath, I start talking, I repeat in a low voice what I've thought out during the preceding night, lilting verses about love and life for example, making it sound as if they were just occurring to me. I take four quick steps to the desk, put a sheet of paper in my typewriter, wait a few seconds, exhale deeply, and type out the prepared sentence with my quick two-finger style. (I gave up typing at random long ago. It sounds completely wrong if what you're writing makes no sense.) When I come to the end of the sentence, I hesitate before typing the period, but then I do so emphatically. Now I keep quiet for a while, then go over what I've written, murmuring it aloud several times as I pull the sheet out, shove my chair back, open the window, and declaim vaguely to the twittering birds. After these empty phrases, voices begin arising from below: the loud enactment of the children's return, grandmother's complaints, mother's concern, grandfather's consolation, in lengthy exchanges. Under the cover of these extraneous sounds, the listener withdraws down the steep steps, descending the stairway quickly to the main living area.

I smell the hot honey milk he's placed in front of my door. I won't take a single sip of it, I'll keep right on coughing. The attacks will probably soon develop into cramps I can't control, followed finally by retching and vomiting, till I choke on my own vomit, and then I'll be dead and quiet.

I lie under my bed and breathe silently through the sleeve of my coat. Days can pass that way. They take turns listening, I hear them whispering when a new one takes over, figuring out what they should do since for days now I haven't touched the food they leave for me on the landing. They poke through the stopped-up keyhole with hairpins and see nothing but the empty chair by the window.

Because I don't eat, I don't need to relieve myself. I get water from a flask hidden under the mattress, my urine flows into a bottle thickly wrapped with socks. Listening keeps me awake, I neither sleep nor snore, no sudden gasps or mumbling dreams betray me. I can keep lying here like a dead man for a long time yet. I have better nerves than they do.

At last they start making noises, run up and down the stairs singing and whistling, throw a party with neighbors in the evening: they drink and carouse and toss pebbles at my window from the garden. At dawn they imitate the sounds of birds, even screech owls, the barking of dogs. They're waiting for me to open the door, to beg for a little peace and quiet with fidgety gestures, my voice tired, hoarse from the long silence. They want to see me, to be shocked at first, then to laugh out loud at the little man in the overcoat, at my pale face, unshaven and unwashed for days. They want to shiver in pleasurable disgust at the emanations from my skin, to retreat before my breath. But I lie still and endure the growing pain of motionlessness until almost noon, when peace descends upon the house. Then I crawl soundlessly beneath the swath cut through my room by the opened keyhole, pull myself up to my desk, and strike the typewriter in the midst of the silence; just one letter, which cuts through the stillness, then a sentence, and finally in rapid succession, interrupted only by sudden short pauses, as if I were seeking a better word, I type all afternoon and through the night as well, typing out the record of what I've heard over the passing days.

And, within the limits of what my suffering mind has been able to store in my memory, there will be no gaps.

## 9.

A man living in an attic apartment, abandoned by his family, decides to end his life, since no one is paying any attention to him. To avoid becoming in death the object of an affection denied to him in life, he wants to die in a way which will make him unworthy of further thought. He plans to commit a crime which will cost him his life. First of all he buys a gun; not because he intends to shoot anyone, and not because he doubts the efficacy of a realistic fake, but because he knows from the movies that only a real gun gives the face of the gunman a truly believable look. Then he seeks out a bank from which it is possible to flee across the roofs of the neighboring buildings to a glass-covered inner courtyard. Here the bullets of his pursuers will strike him, twist him half-way about, and send him crashing through the glass roof into the narrow, empty cobblestone courtyard amid a shower of paper money. But his attempt goes awry. Just as he is in the act of committing the crime, a terrible traffic accident takes place in front of the bank and, except for the man and a woman cashier, all the people in the lobby, customers and tellers alike, rush out onto the street. Faced with the choice of her money or her life, the cashier, a beautiful and elegant woman rendered helpless by fear, stuffs all the money she can get her hands on, including rolls of coins, into the bag held out to her. The man leaves the bank, passes unnoticed through the crowd, and doesn't know what to do next.

Lying on his bed back in the apartment, he decides to spend all the money. He rents a sports convertible and heads for a gambling resort on the Mediterranean. On his way there, descending through a steep and narrow pass in the mountains, he hears the Beatles singing the praises of strawberry fields on the radio. He listens for a while, then closes his eyes, steps on the gas, and drives straight ahead.

## IO.

Jakob, who was making himself unbearable after the death of his mother by the refractory manner in which he approached the fulfillment of his contradictory and hence unfulfillable desires for circumstances which would accord with life as he wished it, found lodgings with a distant relative, an independent woman generally considered quite clever, who lived in a large house in a city to the south, an arrangement engineered by her cousin, a half-brother of his deceased mother, upon whom, as nearest relative and heir to the largest part of the movable goods and property of the family estate, the responsibility of caring for Jakob for the remainder of his life had initially fallen.

This distant relative, if relative is still the word at such a remove, had agreed at once to take Jakob in, and even promised a level of care and love beyond simple financial support, since he was described to her as a friendly, good-natured, and even likeable young man, who, in spite of his odd way of thinking and occasionally acting, took care of himself for the most part and would be content with limited attention. But because, as was commonly suggested, if only behind a shielding hand, she was not only stubborn to the point of perverseness, but also a fiendishly clever business-woman, she recognized the urgency of the request from her barely-known relative and managed to negotiate Jakob's monthly pension upward by citing the rising cost of living in all parts of the country, and particularly in the south, almost doubling what was first offered to her; a success which, she swore secretly to herself, would be used solely for the good of her ward, although she herself was not living in particularly comfortable circumstances, and could have made very good use of a little extra income to help run her household.

The modest savings she had accumulated during her long years abroad, pitting her extreme parsimony against her husband's desire for conspicuous consumption, had been employed to buy this house, which, although it exceeded her needs in every respect, was one of the last of those homes where, even as a little girl, a poor child growing up in this city, she had ardently longed to live; a narrow, three-story brick and frame house, with wooden gables, balconies, and bay-windows, an upper-story entrance beneath a broad stained-glass veranda, and one of those steep roofs, once typical of the region, with high dormer windows and wrought-iron snow rails and gutters. The red house with its white woodwork was set within a half-overgrown garden bordered at the back by a high sandstone wall running along the railroad tracks, and extending forward to the street, where evergreen hedges cut off the deep and spacious lot from view.

Against much well-intentioned advice, the unknown woman purchased the run-down house, which, because it had been taken over by homeless refugees who were managing through cunning and perseverance to avoid formal eviction, was offered at a ridiculously low price, and moved into a small room beneath the eaves, where, since she made no move to drive the uninvited guests from her home, she soon found herself loved and respected by them. And because she accepted as sound and sufficient the argument that those who had settled in her house had, without exception, been there before her, and therefore had a right to remain, while drawing simultaneously the conclusion that each family was responsible for the rooms they occupied, charging them as a group with the care and upkeep of the dangerously decaying house, there soon began an extensive series of repairs and improvements in both the house and the garden, so that when the last of the homeless families finally found lodgings in one of the new buildings in the neighborhood, the property was in a thoroughly respectable condition. Over the following years the owner, expertly advised by her former tenants, many of whom long remained on friendly terms with her, withstood even the most tempting and advantageous offers to sell the house at a large profit, rejecting all plans to tear the old place down to make way for a newer and more suitable building with a steadfastness which finally led the city government, after years of threatening to declare the stubborn woman mentally incompetent and confiscate her property, to designate the house and garden as one of the few characteristic examples of the

wealthy middle-class culture which had once been typical of the city, and thus to declare it worthy of protection and preservation by the state. Against the wishes of
the owner, the house was restored from the ground up,
the garden was cleared, the hedges trimmed, and every
vestige of age and decay removed, so that the traveler
who had been riding in the train past the monotonous
facades of apartment houses for several minutes was
suddenly surprised by the sight of a property that
appeared to him like the setting of some half-forgotten
novel.

And on a wonderful warm afternoon, Jakob was picked
up at the railway station by the woman whom he had
been told at home to call his Aunt, and was brought to
live in her house for the rest of his days.

Jakob, who was standing at an open window as the train
pulled in, recognized her immediately among the
crowd. His aunt, expecting a half-grown young boy,
and not a thirty-year-old, did not become aware of him
until there was no one else waiting on the empty
platform but a man in a heavy, blue-gray, ankle-length
great coat quite unsuited to the season, surrounded by
tightly-tied suitcases and boxes. She stepped up to him,
asked him if he was Jakob, the nephew she'd been
waiting for so eagerly, hugged him firmly when he said
with a laugh that he was, welcomed him, kissed him
without aversion or shame on the red-veined elderly
cheeks of his perspiring child's face, told him just to call
her Auntie, had him leave his luggage standing, called a

porter over, took Jakob by the hand while he was still fiddling about at a loss with his raggedy baggage and led him along the platform, down the stairs, through the spacious hall, and out onto the sunny square where her car was parked, a late-model white Volkswagen convertible. She had the porter load the car, tipped him, waved him off as he fumbled for change, and accepted his bow with a smile. She took the long way around the city through the hills, pointing things out here and there, giving Jakob his first view of his new surroundings.

Jakob moved into the two large rooms his aunt had prepared for him at the rear of the top story looking out over the orchard and the beautiful wall of quarried stone which ran along the railway tracks; she had been told that he loved trains. The shrewd and experienced aunt left the young man mostly to himself for the first few days, giving him time to grow used to his surroundings and the overwhelming happiness he felt, and allowing him to gather his courage to trust her. She helped him arrange the rooms as he wished, offering advice only when asked, and let him have his way when, after initially arranging the furniture and then rearranging it again and again, he finally decided that rather than sleeping in the smaller room in the tower, he would take the larger one with the balcony and its many windows for his bedroom, because the smaller one with all its angles and niches seemed to him more suitable for sorting his papers, while the larger and brighter room seemed perfect for observing the passing trains since on quiet evenings the words from the loudspeaker at the nearby station were carried through the open balcony doors by the west wind.

For hours he stood there watching the traffic on the railroad tracks. He would have liked to have had binoculars, so that he could have read the origins, routes, and destinations from the signboards on the express trains. Nevertheless, he gradually managed to bring the regular flow of rail traffic into harmony with the announcements of the distorted voices from the loudspeaker—a woman's voice by day, and a man's by night—so that he was soon able to state the arrival and departure times of every train before it was announced, where they were coming from, where they were headed, what stations they would stop at along the way, and the connections for the surrounding towns and villages: a game which began to bore him when he no longer lost to the loudspeaker voices except in the case of some unpredictable disruption of the train schedule, and which he abandoned as silly child's play when his aunt, who loved to go to the movies, resumed the afternoon visits to the movies she had given up for his sake, and invited him along.

No experience seemed to him as valuable as sitting alone in the dark among all the people, pursuing the images of stories drawn from the world of true feelings. And so, having found a job as a ticket-taker, usher, and candy vendor in the local cinema through his aunt, who knew the owner, he spent entire days in the movie theater, and learned to love those films in which the plot's alarming twists and turns threaten to make the film end all wrong.

# I I.

Java. Yes, it begins on Java. Close your eyes. And now imagine a flat blue surface. A bright blue, sky blue, azure surface twenty-four meters broad and seven meters high, the totally blue surface of a movie screen. From the upper right hand corner, almost at the edge of the screen, a plane appears, flying at a great height. It gleams in the setting sun, trailing long streams of exhaust. When the plane has almost crossed the screen, and the vapor trails have already begun to dissolve into smaller individual clouds of white, a large bird appears at the lower left, flapping its wings slowly and heavily. Reaching the middle of the screen, it spreads its great wings and sails in broad circles. Now the music sets in. The title superimposed in crass red: The Mystery of the Silver Bird, a Film by Me. The title disappears. The huge bird makes a faster, tighter circle, shakes itself once, twice, and then dips its right wing and plunges from sight. Cut.

An unloaded revolver, its cylinder open, lies upon a wooden table. A tailor's yellow tape measure has been stretched lengthwise down the center of the table, precisely parallel to its edges. Six high-caliber, snub-nosed bullets, each incised with an x, are scattered upon it. The table stands on a brown tile floor, in front of partially open full-length glass doors. Standing in the opening is a man with his back to the camera. He's leaning against the wall with his right shoulder, his left arm stretched out against the window casing. His head is cut off by the upper edge of the camera frame. He's wearing light-gray flannel trousers. His bare upper torso is deeply tanned. On his left wrist is a heavy watch. At this very moment, the second hand stops. The watch shows ten to eleven, but outside it could be any time of day. The wall of glass opens onto a blue sea without shore or horizon. The man stands for some time without moving. The only sound is that of small waves breaking on a stony beach. From far away, but clearly audible and growing in intensity, comes the roar of a high-flying jet. For a few moments it drowns out the steady slapping of the waves, then it fades away. The man pushes off from the window frame with his right shoulder, drops his left arm tiredly, and shoves his hands into his pockets. Hunching his shoulders, he takes a deep breath, as if seized by a sudden pain. He releases his breath, turns around, and approaches the table. His face comes into view. It's Franco Nero. He hasn't shaved for days, and his eyes are blue as the sea. He picks up the shells from the table, weighs them in the palm of his hand, then places them at regular intervals along the tape measure. Bending over the highly polished surface of the table, he spreads his hands flat upon it. A narrow, pale band is visible on his right ring finger. The telephone emits a low buzz. A barely perceptible tension runs through the outspread fingers. The telephone buzzes five times. Then the hands leave the table.

41

The man moves out of the camera frame. The hand-prints evaporate from the outside in, as his voice is heard replying to inaudible instructions: yes . . . yes . . . no . . . no.

Bird's-eye view: a mountainous, stony, sparsely-covered landscape in all shades from ocher to red, through which a pale yellow sandy path winds. Along this path a heavy blue motorcycle races at breakneck speed, drawing a long trail of dust behind it. Now and then it disappears into a depression or behind a hill, and then all you can see is the bright, whirling cloud of dust. No music, no sound of a motor. You don't even hear the wind among the rock formations glowing in the evening sun. As the seconds pass, you wait ever more expectantly for the cut to a close-up of the blue-clad figure on the motorcycle, unrecognizable under the lowered visor of the blue crash-helmet. But the cut doesn't come. After a sweeping, half-circular curve along a nearly dried-out riverbed which the camera follows in its flight, the coast comes into view, with an indescribably blue sea. Atop a gentle hill just above the point where the river enters the sea stands a white house in a broad, carefully-tended garden which lies like an oasis in the midst of the desolate landscape. Now the camera closes in for the first time. The path merges into a white gravel lane, shaded by tall eucalyptus trees, onto which the motorcyclist turns at this moment, etching a long sharp skid mark. The rider comes to a stop and dismounts next to a Ferrari-red Ferrari which is parked in a large courtyard fronting the white wooden ve-randa. You can tell it's a woman by the way she moves.

She takes off her helmet, shakes out her long, blond hair, which flows down as if it has never been held beneath a helmet before, wipes her sweaty face with her left hand, leaving a dusty smear down her forehead across her eyes, nose, and mouth, and as she takes a deep breath and unzips her leather outfit with a jerk which seems tired for all its energy, you recognize Catherine Deneuve, and she's more beautiful than ever before. The way she goes up the narrow stairs, strips off her leather overalls with apparent nonchalance and tosses them across the balustrade, you've never seen anything like it—the way she smiles at Franco Nero, who steps out from the twilight of the house through the wide-open doors of the veranda, melts into his embrace in her inimitable style, closing her eyes. She calls him Paul, he says Catherine. They stand motionless for some time in the quickly gathering tropical twilight. And later, re-membering this image, it will seem to you as if your own life ceased for those wonderful forty-five seconds in which nothing happened. She pulls away from his shoulder and lets her head fall back very slowly. With this gesture the scene fades to Paul's bedroom. In extreme close-up: his face, half buried in the pillows. He's asleep. Music sets in, taking up the calm rhythm of his breath. Through the diamond-weave of the window shades bright morning light enters the room, casting a strictly geometrical pattern of light and dark across Paul's face, the pillows, the entire room. Sharply etched within the bright lozenges, each pore, each whisker, each eyelash on the lids which twitch almost impercep-tibly at irregular intervals. After a long pause he opens his eyes without blinking. Paul's eye fills the screen, its pupil gradually contracting. Then the camera pulls away at the same compellingly slow pace. The walls, the ceiling, the floor of the room come into view, covered by the sharp distorting contours of the diamond pattern. Crowded side-by-side upon the walls, standing in the corners, crouching in the bookcases, lying on the floor, carved wooden masks and figures from an unknown, distant culture. Their eyes, of inlaid mother-of-pearl, turquoise, polished coral, gleam in the twilight of the darkened room. Sudden close-up of a gaping mouth. Behind grimacing boar's teeth a thick dark tongue.

Cut to a large mouth, laughing loudly. Thus we meet Paipietie, a dark-skinned native of the islands, a giant of a man with a thick mop of hair who emphasizes everything he says with a rich series of gestures. And what am I supposed to do? asks Paipietie, be your driver? No, says Paul, you'll be the interpreter, if there's anything to interpret. My people speak a thousand tongues, you surely know that. The island's uninhabited. What do you want us along for? In case it's not uninhabited. Oh, and then dumb little Paipietie is supposed to tell them all the good things the clever white man can do. Dat's good, dat's verry good, massa. You can drop that stuff. Do you think I like doing this? The two men cross a huge parking lot filled with cars but entirely devoid of people; bumper to bumper and not a person in sight except for the two of them. It's blindingly hot. They go up to an old Chevy taxi painted bright yellow and metallic blue and get in. Leaning on the horn, Paipietie drives at high speed through an unbelievable snarl of traffic. All the windows are rolled down. Paul sits beside him with his arm out the window, patting the roof of the car with the flat of his hand in three-four time. On the dashboard stands a small stuffed alligator; two plastic shrunken heads dangle from the rear-view mirror. Who else is coming along? Howard. Howard? That asshole all right. What's it all about? Uranium? Something like that. The old man will tell you all about it. Sounds like it's top-secret. He didn't say anything to me on the phone either. Crappy dialogue. Dialogue doesn't really have a place in films. It's always either too early or too late. Either it gives everything away in advance, or it explains things we've already caught on to long ago. A film that's any good doesn't need dialogue. Who cares whether Catherine Deneuve calls Franco Nero Paul? Do you care about people's names in films? I don't. I think it's ridiculous. Dialogue only works in films when what's being said has nothing whatever to do with what's being shown, when it occurs at the wrong moment. When people speak simply because they do speak to one another, just as they walk, sleep, run, and fight with one another. At any rate there's no dialogue in my film. Sounds yes, but no words. Say for example proximity, or say distance. Nothing. The only real words left are images in films.

You see in quick succession two infrared aerial views of an oval island from the same perspective, taken from almost directly overhead. They flash against a black background, rear-projected onto the slide screen, and not a single ray of light cuts through the whirling smoke which fills the room in which six, no seven, men are sitting. Four we don't know and won't see again, Paipietie and Franco Nero, and up in front, standing at an angle to the screen, Trevor Howard, with a penlight in his hand. You only see the room and the people during the three seconds between slides when the screen turns bright white and everything is suddenly illuminated by the glare. It turns dark again, and now the island is offered to your gaze for a longer time. You have to study the image carefully, since the colors are totally artificial: yellow, red, blue. The sea is yellow, the forests are various shades of red, the mountain peaks are blue with sharply outlined patches of dark violet which are now being indicated with the little arrow of the penlight. Here, says Trevor Howard, making rough circles around the violet patches with the little arrow. The following slides are in natural color. The sea is blue, almost inky, the surf breaks whitely on the reef, lagoons in all shades of turquoise against pearl-white sand beaches, the forests dark green, the mountain slopes lighter green, the rock cliffs gray-brown. The last slides now in quick succession, the island from an increasingly lower altitude. Finally a hilly forest fills the screen, one treetop next to the other, thick, so thick that it seems you couldn't even fall through them. You've seen no sign of a settlement, no village, no fields, no paths.

A marine assault boat takes Howard, Paul, and Paipietie to a deserted island beach. The beach is beautiful as only tropical beaches can be. The landing ramp at the bow splashes down. The three men in camouflage outfits, carrying everything they need for a tropical expedition, including boxes of scientific instruments, run across the pearl-white beach in a crouch and fall to the ground beneath the thick bushes at the edge of the jungle. Paul gives a terse signal, the landing ramp is raised, the boat takes off trailing a mighty wake, and disappears behind a spit of land. Although the three men have only run about a hundred yards, they're breathing heavily. Their faces are drenched with sweat. They listen for a while, straining their ears. But since nothing can be heard but the distant sound of the surf on the reef beyond the lagoon, their faces relax. Paul slips out of his rucksack, straightens up, pats his sweat-soaked shirt pockets for cigarettes and matches, and the three men smoke, while above them, in the wind-whipped crowns of the coconut palms, the long-tailed monkeys take up their games again with annoyed shrieks.

So. And now come scene after scene after scene depicting their laborious progress through the jungle mountains. Images of danger and exhaustion—you've seen them a hundred times before. How the three men cross a rushing river filled with rapids on a homemade raft; how one of them saves the other's life with a lightning blow of his machete, severing the darting head of a poisonous snake from its brightly-marked body as it angles in to attack from a low-hanging branch; how they slowly wade through a deep swamp, trying to make as little noise as possible, holding their packs above their heads, tortured by swarms of mosquitoes, the brownish-yellow eye slits of voracious alligators peering at them from the stagnant water; how they pitch camp at last, exhausted and covered with mud, beneath the shade of the final tree on the edge of the bare, scorching upland plains, sharing the last of their water in tiny sips; how they cavort beneath a waterfall in the tropical forest like unruly children, washing the dregs of the exhausting days from their naked bodies; how the native, holding his gun in readiness, places the tips of his index and ring fingers beneath his curled tongue, imitating the call of the female in heat to lure the black panther that has been circling the camp for several nights, and how he kills it with a single shot in mid-leap; how a poisonous thorn tears a deep, bloody flesh wound through a shirt, a wound which festers and saps all strength as the days pass; how the men, wrapped in their blankets, stare with weary eyes at the night sky in which the Southern Cross sparkles; how the next day the stronger man takes over the burden of the one weakened by fever; and of course you see what none of the actors do—for they move through the film as if they are in totally unfamiliar territory—you see that all this is being watched by dark eyes set in faces painted red and yellow.

Howard is at the end of his strength. He collapses, babbling about birds of death circling above him. Paul and Paipietie make a stretcher and drag him along upland. The jungle begins to thin out, turns into a gentle, hilly meadowland. The grass is almost chest high. It makes walking difficult. They reach the crest and look down across a broad, flat plateau. A plain surface five times the size of a soccer field has been cut into the darkly swaying grass, as if it had been mowed, with square corners and sharply defined edges, a bright green field, smooth as ceramic, totally senseless, in the middle of the wilderness, not cultivated, not a playing field, no building anywhere, no sign of life. Nothing.

Paul trains his binoculars on the edge of the forest, the horizon of the grasslands, and the mountains which rise again beyond the plateau, the steep rock formations. The camera follows the slowly revolving circle of the binoculars. Stillness, peace, nothing more.

Paul motions for Paipietie to pick up Howard's stretcher again and nods in the direction they should follow to reach the field. They bend over, lift the stretcher with Trevor sleeping uneasily upon it, and straighten up.

Cut to a close-up of a dark face striped across the forehead and the cheek bones with parallel lines of yellow and red, a nose-bone, white feathers in a black mop of hair, dangling earlobes. The camera moves quickly on. Above grass swaying more strongly now, another dark head, another brightly-painted face, and another, and another. The camera cranes upward and tracks back in the same motion, showing the group as a whole in a long shot. In the middle Paul and Paipietie. Between them they hold the stretcher—Howard is lying totally motionless now—in a closed circle of twenty small, dark-skinned men armed with bows and arrows. Each of them is holding an arrow pointed downwards from a bow stretched tight, hip-high. The image is held; nothing can be heard but the sound of the wind in the grass; nothing moves but the wind.

Hesitantly, having difficulty getting the focus right, the camera approaches for a medium shot of a few of the dark painted faces. The first is marked by a bright red toothbrush extending from ear to ear, piercing the septum of his nose, passing through an ugly, scarred opening. The second is wearing a green ball-point pen beneath his nose and champagne corks in his enlarged earlobes, a third has bored through his nose just below eye-level with a large, polished brass screw, and rivets of various size and color have been passed through his ears. The fourth man is wearing the old frame of a pair of eyeglasses in his nose; the lid of a Nivea jar dangles from that of the sixth, partially covering his mouth; the seventh has inserted rolled-up yogurt lids through holes in his nostrils. The one with the toothbrush, apparently the leader, since he also wears the most extravagant set of feathers, motions for the white men to follow him. Escorted by the black warriors they go down into a dale at the edge of the open field; a dozen circular grass huts stand in a half-circle around an open square with a long-house made of woven reeds. In the square women and children stare silently at the approaching men. There's no scuffling, no cries, no crowding.

The strange tribe takes in the three exhausted men with friendly reserve. They receive food and drink, and a hut to sleep in. The three recover quickly and start to work. Trevor Howard explores the hills. He gathers soil and rock samples, surveys the land, draws maps, makes long lists. He's so busy gathering his topological and geological information that he doesn't even notice he's being followed at every step by dark spies. Paul wanders in what seems an aimless manner through the village and the surrounding area. He observes and lets himself be observed, he paces off the length and breadth of the open field, counting each step to himself. He watches the children at play, the women at work, the men in their long gesture-rich conversations. He sits before the hut for a long time, writing and drawing what he sees in a book bound in gray. Paipietie, although he understands not a single word of the tribal language laden with vowel shifts, quickly finds his way into its gestures, motions, signs, and spends much of his time with the men. Paipietie's forays into the exchanges in sign language always occasion a good deal of laughter. Late in the afternoon the men gather in the village square. They draw fresh stripes across each other's foreheads, red and yellow earth colors mixed with saliva, and stick hawk feathers in each other's hair. Then they arrange themselves quietly and solemnly into a procession-like line, leave the village, and follow a narrow jungle path up the mountain. Paipietie, who wants to join them, is turned back firmly. The men disappear silently into the bush. The women pull the children into the huts and let down screens of woven grass to cover the entrances. A profound silence has set in around Paul and Paipietie, suddenly broken by a cursing Trevor, who carries a heavy sack filled with broken chunks of rock up to them and drops it at their feet. All high-grade positive, he says excitedly, but with a brusque gesture Paipietie orders him to speak more softly. It all tests positive, Trevor whispers. Paipietie just looks at him. Then he hurries across the square to the long-house at the edge of the broad field. He opens the door and slips inside. The other two follow him.

In the long, low shadowy hut the three men stand at a loss, amazed, amidst a jumble of items carefully arranged by color: plastic objects, some hanging in bundles from the roof; scraps of tarpaulin and rigging; broken bits of crates, buckets, and barrels; old packing materials with and without address labels; torn sacks and bags—blue with blue, yellow with yellow, red with red. Standing on woven grass floor mats, also arranged by color, are tin cans and bottles, canisters, cups, boxes and receptacles of every sort, lined up by size. Upon an altar-like table against the narrow end of the building opposite the entrance, in reed baskets lined with white feathers lie three light bulbs, a radio tube, a neon rod, and, embedded in blue feathers, a doll's head with long blond hair and closed eyes. Paipietie lifts the small, smiling head, cautiously, almost reverently, and click click, with just that momentary delay, the shining blue eyes open. These two small mechanical sounds make him catch his breath. In the distance you hear the low roar of a jet flying at a great height.

So far, so good. Everything's in place. In a manner of speaking, the story can plunge into tragedy in free fall. The following evening Howard, Paul, and Paipietie sneak after the procession of men. They watch from the thick bushes as the natives, in an acute angle opening toward the southwest, sit down on the summit of a cliff which falls away steeply toward the forest and bow repeatedly toward the setting sun. The one with the red toothbrush, the chief or medicine man, starts a solemn song. Sun worshipers, Howard whispers; Paul shakes his head. Paipietie seems paralyzed. Suddenly the natives fall to their faces on the ground. Each of them places his head between the slightly spread legs of the one in front of him. All of them hold their arms at a slight angle. The red stripes painted on their backs, arms, and legs now form a magic sign pointing in a direction the three men follow involuntarily with their eyes. The acute triangle points directly toward the bright, broad field in the grassy plain beneath them. Cut.

The sky opens before you. Lower left the setting sun, from the upper right a jet flying very high, leaving a long vapor trail which dissolves into small pink-white clouds. It's the evening flight from Singapore to Los Angeles. When the sound of the plane has faded away the men stand up, placing their arms on each other's shoulders to form a tight circle. They lean their foreheads together and sway against each other, turning in a slow circle to a gloomy sing-song. Paipietie stands up, pushes away Paul's hands as he tries to restrain him, and joins the circle of quietly mourning men. Cut.

Exterior. Night. Paipietie and the head priest are sitting by the fire. Around them stand, sit, crouch the natives, men, women, and children, far enough away that the camera shows them only as shadows in the flickering light. Among them, tall and light-skinned, stand Howard and Paul. They watch the hands of the chief telling a story in wondrously minute gestures, a story you grasp at once. Every day the great silver bird flies across the world from horizon to horizon. One day he will land on this island, there on the field where the grass has been leveled, and carry all the villagers to the Land of Happiness with its marvelous objects—so many mysterious pieces of which have been washed up by the sea onto the shore—objects permeated with the deep and resonant power of hope. The great silver bird will come and save them all, take them all to that distant land beyond distress and death. And life there will be like the strange material from which holy things are made: not hard like stone, not perishable like grass, but eternal, flexible, multi-colored, and indescribably, mysteriously beautiful. Cut.

Exterior. Day. Wide-angle. Paul, Howard, and Paipietie are standing in the middle of the broad landing field. Howard is talking loudly and excitedly. Paul stands with his back to the camera, bending over slightly, his hands in his pockets, his head lowered. Paipietie stands without moving, his arms folded on his chest, his hands in his armpits, looking left beyond the picture frame, his head turned away from Howard. You're too far away, you can't understand Howard's stream of words. Subtitles, running rapidly in computer script from right to left without punctuation, with no relationship to the succession of gestures. Let's give them what their crazy religion wants let's play god we'll get an airbus to land here and take them to their plastic paradise it doesn't come any cheaper what do they need some wooden huts at the edge of a dump free meatballs and potatoes every day and a few decorative shopping bags we can have the air-traffic rerouted there'll be a bit of trouble with the immortality thing but so what. Paipietie turns to Howard and slaps him in the face, not too softly, not too hard. The subtitles are gone, you can't read what Howard hisses to the black man before he withdraws slowly toward the huts, trying for Henry Fonda's dignity. Suddenly he starts to run, and before anyone grasps what he means to do, he runs up to the long-house, snatches his lighter from his pocket and sets the temple of holy objects on fire before black hands can pull him away. In an instant the reed building is ablaze, burning brightly and clearly at first, then billowing thick black smoke.

At the edge of the landing field the men sit in a long row before the burned-out long-house. Among them Paipietie, naked, with red and yellow stripes under his eyes. They're all staring at a single point. Out in the leveled field Howard lies face-down on the ground, spread-eagled. His hands and feet are tied to pegs. Naked, the sun is directly above him. You don't need a close-up; you know how he looks. Flocks of birds are sitting in the trees at the jungle's edge. The first few fly over, land beside Howard, hop about him, hack at him with long necks. Then you hear the sound of a helicopter above the jungle. With a storm of cries, huge flocks of birds take wing, darkening the sky for an instant; behind them an attack helicopter comes into the picture, just above the tree tops, circles once, and settles in the landing field. The men have jumped up and are standing at a loss. The women and children emerge from the huts and run toward the helicopter, shouting and waving. Close-up of the perplexed faces of the helicopter crew behind the dirty bubble. Shift to close-up of black faces, crying out in ecstasy, tears streaming down, enraptured smiles, outstretched hands, figures stumbling forward in slow motion. Cut to the helicopter. The crew confers excitedly, the pilot revs the engine, the rotor blades spin more rapidly. Dust whirls up in clouds. But nothing stops the natives, they run with twisted faces as if they're running for their lives. From the helicopter comes machine-gun fire, a few stagger, crumple, fall to the ground, drag themselves on. Amidst the uproar and screams a sudden sound-cut: white noise. The first natives have reached the rising machine, clutch at the skids, a few can't hang on, fall to the ground. Wild machine-gun fire from the helicopter. Rigid with terror, Paul watches the massacre from the village square. Paipietie is struck in the forehead by a bullet in the midst of a terrible scream. Overloaded, the helicopter has trouble gaining altitude, turns slowly on its own axis, loses altitude, a hundred hands stretch out toward it, seize it, hang on to it wherever two fingers can catch hold. The machine rears up under full power, flips over, splits apart, and explodes in a fireball. You watch it happen as if through a thick sheet of bullet-proof glass. Everything moves slowly, as in some other medium, without a single sound, in merciless silence.

Paul, the lone survivor, stands on a high, steep cliff far above the trees. He stands there for a long time, very straight, his arms hanging loosely at his sides. He looks quite handsome in the glare of the setting sun. His eyes are totally empty and blue like the sky, in which at this moment, from the right, near the top edge of the screen, a tiny plane flies into view. Paul slowly removes his clothes. He stands naked for a time, staring toward the plane. Then he spreads his arms and falls forward off the high cliff. Very slowly, turning a few times, his body falls toward the dark forest. Just as he plunges through the black, shadowy line of the tree tops a large bird floats up from the same spot in a broad circle without moving its wings. The wind carries the bird higher and higher. Rising in an expanding spiral it approaches the line of the plane's flight, calmly, as a matter of course. Bird and plane meet at a tiny point and coalesce in the clear evening sky. The birdplane continues off the screen. The vapor trail dissolves into tiny individual clouds that quickly dissipate. The End.

I have three other endings, but this is the most beautiful.

# 12.

On Occuli Sunday, the 17th of March, a date he never forgot, because he attended a matineé of Jean-Luc Godard's second film *Vivre sa vie* at the local French Institute that morning, in the original version and without subtitles, Jakob, returning home after a long detour just in time for lunch, thoroughly soaked by an icy rain, discovered his aunt, seemingly lifeless, lying at the foot of the stairs. He lifted the softly-breathing body carefully, carried her upstairs, amazed at her lightness, laid her on the bed, undressed her, examined her for injuries, discovered none with the exception of a swollen left foot, regarded her childlike frailty for some time, and pulled the coverlet over her when she started to shiver.

It was the first time Jakob had been in his aunt's bedroom, for he had known from the start—even though nothing had ever been said about it; it hadn't been expressly forbidden—that he was not to enter her apartment. And since it seemed important to his aunt that each of them have a separate living space in the house (beyond the rooms they shared on the ground floor, the kitchen, the dining room, and the winter garden), and since she had never called him to her room

and only visited him in his own rooms when he invited her, he had resisted the temptation to examine her unlocked apartment even when she was away, in spite of the fact that he had been strongly drawn to ever since a late summer afternoon when, standing in the darkened stairwell, he had observed a mysterious radiance through the crack of her slightly open door. The walls of the three sparsely-furnished but richly carpeted rooms—a living room, a bedroom, and a dressing room, connected by open sliding glass doors so that they formed a suite along the entire front of the first floor—were completely covered with mirrors of all shapes and sizes; from the width of a hand to the height of a man, round, oval, tall and narrow, square, rectangular, framed in black, red-brown, honey-yellow, carved, flat, inlaid, matte, or polished wood, or rimmed in gold or silver: Jakob saw himself splintered wide eyed into a hundred facets, sitting on the edge of aunt's bed.

When he stood up to draw the curtains from the windows so that more light could enter the shaded room, he suddenly found himself between two mirrors hanging at a slight angle to one another on opposite walls; his body, multiplied into two infinite rows of images, became increasingly smaller until it disappeared.

Jakob drew back in shock and didn't dare try game again. At that moment his aunt awoke, too confused and apparently unaware of where she was what had happened to her, babbling about galloping horses pressing around her, flocks of screaming

she sat up without realizing she was naked and vomited foam over Jakob's outstretched hands. Whimpering from the pain in her head she sank back onto the pillows and wept through closed eyes.

Helpless with fear, Jakob called a doctor, who, after what seemed a very cursory examination of the woman who had now completely regained her senses, declared that she had a concussion and a sprain: he ordered her to stay in bed, keep the room dark, get plenty of sleep, and then showed Jakob how to bandage her sprained foot tightly with cold cloths to relieve the pain and prevent swelling.

Jakob nursed his aunt skillfully and attentively, kept clean cloths and ice water ready for the bandages, shook out the bedding and pillows several times a day, cut a sturdy cane from the hazelnut bush in the garden for her to lean on when she had to leave the bed, fixed her breakfast in the morning, which they ate together at her bedside, cooked thin soups which, to their surprise and his joy turned out to be excellent, provided her, since she was an avid smoker, with the carefully-controlled ration of cigarettes proposed by the doctor, and since she wasn't supposed to strain her eyes, read novels aloud to her in the afternoon and early evening; and while she slept he did the housekeeping as quietly as possible, went shopping on his own, was usually back from the city by the time she was awake, and always had something for her, candy, flowers, perfume, a novel.

When her condition had finally improved to the point where she could laugh again without immediately falling prey to a headache, he entertained her with funny stories and all kinds of silliness, finally telling and showing her how frightened he had been on the day of her fall when he saw himself multiplied to infinity by the mirrors on opposite sides of the room; how in the meantime it amused him that all the Jakobs in those endless rows, even the most distant one barely the size of his thumb, had to imitate every face, every grotesque position he, the one and only, yes as he could now rightly be called, the true Jakob, chose to assume; and that he had decided to interrupt all his other studies, no matter how important they were, until he had deciphered the mystery of this no doubt illusory infinity. And he recalled that he had already confronted this mystery once as a child, when he held a jar of shoe polish in his hand with the picture of a frog king on the lid, holding a jar of shoe polish with a picture of a frog king on the lid, holding a jar of shoe polish with a picture of a frog king on the lid, holding a jar of shoe polish; until on the last jar the frog king was only a dot that might equally well have been a tiger king.

After some hesitation the aunt agreed to let him borrow as many mirrors as he thought necessary to carry out his experiments, reminding him that every mirror was valuable and would have to be returned to its place, for although she was worried about losing irreplaceable pieces, her ward's earnest enthusiasm for the study of her own greatest passion seemed worthy of encouragement. Jakob posed before the mirrors in his tower room under every sort of light; naked, dressed entirely in black, draped in bright-colored shawls, changing his posture suddenly or shifting so slowly that the motion became almost imperceptible; and since he took careful notes on each position, he discovered that the reflected image was determined solely by the angle of the mirror to the object, and that only the reflection of a reflected image produced the amazing and at the same time frightening illusion of infinity. Disappointed on the one hand that the overpowering impression of endlessness could be produced by such simple means, but relieved by the certainty he had gained that his own image in mirrors was limited to forms which he himself determined (he had been waiting in tense anxiety for the moment when, if only for a fraction of a second, he would see himself naked in a mirror as he stood before it fully dressed), he reported to his aunt, who asked how his experiments were going, that the nature of the reflection—referring to the notes and sketches he had made during his investigations—depended solely on the relationship of the mirror to an object, or the object to a mirror, and that the reflection of an image in a third mirror by means of a second followed a rule which, once grasped, was quite simple. An object is reflected into a third mirror at exactly the same angle at which the object is reflected from mirror one into mirror two, and a third line can be drawn to mirror four and a fourth to mirror five and so on. Even given the smallest conceivable angle, it would be possible, with enough mirrors of the same size, to reach a point at which the image from the last mirror would be superimposed exactly upon that of the first. This rule could be demonstrated most strikingly with a burning candle in a darkened room. The angle at which the candlelight strikes the mirror— he used the term angle of incidence—was exactly the same as the angle at which the light would be reflected. The angle of reflection seemed to him too repetitive for this second term, while angle of deflection sounded too much like a sports term, so he had settled on angle of coincidence to match angle of incidence. In short, the angle of incidence corresponded exactly, in each and every case, to the angle of coincidence. At zero angle, and by zero he meant two mirrors situated precisely opposite one another, nothing seemed to happen at all. Only after thinking about it for some time did he realize that a reflected image showed the reflected object in what could be called a full angle, so that the reflection of the reflection was reflected upon itself. It may be noted in passing that he was particularly happy to have seen himself as others saw him for the first time in his life in the reflected reflection. The rest had been child's play. A fraction beyond zero, at the smallest angle, the images repeated themselves endlessly, as had been demon- strated, and if you placed your head in the line of reflection, you seemed to see yourself disappearing into infinity. If anyone wanted to count them, he would eventually reach the largest possible number. But since he now knew the rules, he himself was not interested in this number; someone else could figure that out. Infinite reflection in its purest form was of course beyond actual sight, conceptual only: the dark of an endlessly repeating void when two mirrors were placed face to face.

The aunt regarded Jakob silently for a long time after he had closed his notebook, and finally said in a low voice, softly drawing out the syllables of the words, that what impressed her most about his work, which in general she thought extraordinarily clever, was the unprecedented realization that in the end all mysteries turn out to be true, and for that reason she would show him another way of looking at the reflected world some day. Jakob greeted this announcement with a small laugh which was intended to show how little further interest he had in a riddle once it was solved, and his aunt, although she understood his laugh correctly, seemed in no way annoyed. Instead she joined in his laughter, leaned on his arm, took him into the kitchen, opened a cupboard in which keys to all the doors in the house were hanging in labelled bunches, and after describing them all, invited him to explore the house from top to bottom, including the garden house and the sheds, and she made it clear she was not excluding her own rooms.

Jakob roamed through the house for days, sat for hours in the attic before opened trunks and chests stuffed with clothes of all colors and styles, boots and shoes for every purpose, suitcases and bags for every conceivable trip, with boxes, cases, and packages tied with string which proved to contain newspaper clippings, papers, letters, and documents in various languages; he found drawings and paintings, packets of photographs and prints of landscapes, views of cities, houses, groups of people, individuals, portraits, which seemed to him both familiar and strange at the same time. He was overwhelmed

by an oppressive feeling that time had stopped—
something he had often experienced as a child—a feeling which grew into intense confusion when he found
photos in a blue envelope of a young man who, although there was something foreign about his ap-
pearance—with his widely spaced, strangely shaped
eyes, the narrow, sharp nose between the high cheek-
bones, and the scar across the low forehead—looked
exactly like him, as he knew now that his own face was
familiar to him as was no other from his long sessions in
the mirror: he resembled him in every detail, to a hair.
The sepia photographs showed him as a uniformed
equestrian on a show horse in the midst of a triple jump;
driving an open car in a trench coat, with a leather
helmet and goggles; as a gymnast in white, laughing
with fellow athletes, in a striped pullover, his hands
shoved in both pockets of light-colored, roomy trousers, next to a young woman in a flowered dress whom
Jakob recognized immediately; as a bicycle racer, his
cap turned backwards; in evening dress with a large
family on the front steps of a country estate; in a pilot's
uniform leaning against the wing of a moth-balled
fighter plane under camouflage nets; as a mountain
climber in full gear, standing on a snow-capped peak
below the summit cross, an ice-ax in his right hand, the
rope—apparently attached to the friend photographing
him—in his left, his eyes protected from the glare of the
sun by dark glasses. Finally, a postcard-size portrait
photo, a close-up in half profile, gazing solemnly and
bright-eyed toward a distant goal, his neck tightly
encircled by the high collar of a uniform, on the tabs of
which a lieutenant's star was gleaming.

Jakob put all the photos back in the envelope except for the one of the mountain climber, put the envelope back in its box, the box back in the suitcase, the suitcase back in the wardrobe, and locked the wardrobe, avoiding as he did so his own image in the mirror on the middle door. He went to his room in the tower, pulled the curtains across the small windows, placed the photo under the desk lamp, and looked at it for a long time. He would have liked nothing better in life than a pair of goggles like mountain climbers wear to keep from going snow-blind when they cross fields of old snow: a pair of glasses made for glaciers, with circular black lenses fixed solidly in metal rims, with flexible frames that wrap around the ears, and a rubber band around the back of the head for extra security and a tighter fit, plus leather flaps that extend to the temples to protect the eyes from the side glare, enclosing on both sides the darkened vision, focusing the eyes on the next step of the route, so that in order to take note of what's around you, you have to make a clear decision to look in a new direction.

The next day Jakob started searching for evidence about this person's life beyond the photographs. He found stacks of letters which might be from him, tied with blue ribbons, stamped in distant lands, written in a strange script; found coats and jackets, sweaters and items from a uniform, shoes and hats like the man was wearing in the photographs, but everything he tried on was made for a larger and heavier person. In oversized riding boots, in overalls too large and too long for him, a pilot's cap on his head the rim of which reached down to his eyebrows, he regarded himself in the mirror of the wardrobe door, and was suddenly overcome by a strange uneasiness he couldn't suppress even by quickly reeling off the rules of reflection. It seemed to him that the space in the mirror was expanding with every breath he took. It was scarcely noticeable at first, but after a few deep breaths he saw quite clearly that his image was receding. He jerked the wardrobe door open, turning away the mirror. Trying to breathe as shallowly as possible, he returned the scattered things to the wardrobe, in no particular order. When he closed the mirrored door he was a tiny figure in the distance. He shut his eyes and felt his way to the attic door, fearing one more breath would prevent him from reaching it; holding his breath he left the room and went downstairs to his aunt's apartment. When his aunt saw the state he was in, she motioned for him to draw near, took him in her arms, caressed him, kissed him, murmured over and over that her little Jakob had come home at last, pressed him against her, awakening in him a burning desire to which she responded with passion. They lay together for a long time, exchanging soft words of love. When it grew dark, she sat up, cradled his head in her lap, and began telling him everything from the first day she saw him and immediately loved him. And while she spoke to him in various languages, stopping now and then to chide herself gently for her poor memory, for forgotten names and concepts, the mirrors were illuminated one by one, revealing images to illustrate her stories, deserts and white cities, snow-capped mountains, burning plains, flocks of birds in storms, horse races, duels, steamships in river deltas, urban palaces and country estates, Swiss villages, nomadic caravans, battle-grounds and gardens, devastated fields, boulevards and avenues, horsemen, pilots, dancing savages, soldiers and abandoned wives, mothers and young girls, gamblers, country priests, prisoners in bare cells, parties under awnings, figures in various dress on the streets and squares, in parks and quiet rooms, on stairways and behind barricades, and the faces of many men and women in whose expressions memory alone seemed present. He tired, she spoke more softly, whispering him into sleep, fell silent as he dozed off, and let the pictures fade.

From then on they slept together and loved one another each day. In the evenings they told each other stories of their own and other lives and encountered in the images of distant times and places experiences they thought they had forgotten and people long since declared missing and rooms believed forever destroyed by fire. At times they were seen strolling hand in hand in the garden at night, and they could be heard talking softly, and laughing, and crying. They walked together like mother and child, and yet were man and wife.

# 13.

Jakob lived happily for three years in this way. On his birthday he revealed to the woman that he was Moy. When, in spite of all her entreaties, he refused to her horror to retract what he couldn't retract, she no longer wished to share her bed and table with him, and when he tried to overcome her resistance by a half-hearted show of force, she exiled him to his original rooms in the upper story, forbade him to ever enter her apartment again, which he would henceforth find locked, threatened to shoot him if he should ever try to touch her again, declared that from then on he could only leave the house with her permission, which he would have to obtain through the closed door, indicated the times of day he would find his meals placed on the middle landing of the staircase, and announced her intention to have the police evict him from the house if he ever disobeyed a single one of her conditions.

Jakob said nothing, asked nothing, explained nothing; he went up to his room, seemingly unaffected, opened the door to his balcony, stepped out, listened to the loudspeaker, matched its every word, followed the arriving and departing trains, and sent those traveling to distant destinations picture postcards in his head, to which however he added a postscript, that he would never again accept anyone as his guardian. Then he closed the balcony door, pulled the curtains across it, lay down on the bed and asked that the pain stop biting at him. But since the pain bit him like a quickly growing family of spiders, he stood up, searched through the entire house, and tried to ease it by swallowing every pill, powder, and medicinal syrup he could find.

Jakob awoke with a strong thirst for cold blackberry tea in a strange white bed in a strange white room. He found himself attached to instruments and with both hands tied to the railings of the bed. He called out for Moy, but Moy wasn't there.

## 14.

And falling asleep, the years suddenly faded, past was present, and you were back when it seemed all movement had finally ceased. Father sitting stock-still in his room; Hermann standing motionless, bent over the account books; Mother frozen in the kitchen, her hands immersed in the cooling rinse water; and in the morning, when you awoke, she too would move again. You imagined the three Brigittes, Sexton Beck with his fiddle, the dog and the cows in the stall, all frozen in place, and it seemed perfectly natural to you that nothing could move without you and that there was no motion beyond your sight. All right, it was conceivable that Hermann might have written in the account books with his red and blue copy pens, might have lifted a hand to turn a page, that Mother might have wrung out her dishtowel, wiped the back of her hand across her forehead to push back her hair, the dog might have stretched, the Sexton might have played Praise God From Whom All Blessings Flow, but it made no sense.

And, you must remember, Snow White always seemed more than a simple fairy tale to me.

Sometimes you were afraid that you too would find yourself unable to move. Then you would spread your fingers, roll your head back and forth on the pillow, open and close your eyes, and the senselessness of these small movements seemed to prove that you were right in suspecting that everything that happened, even the most insignificant things, revolved around you.

A bell-jar on the cherry wood commode in the living room enclosed a delicate white porcelain figure: a sexless child lying on its back with both hands stretched out toward a golden butterfly that had alighted on its right foot, which was pointed toward the sky. Mother said she thought this little figure was the perfect image of earthly happiness; and because you were so clumsy, she issued a strict order that you were never to touch it. One day, as you were breaking this commandment by lifting the bell-jar, you struck the figurine with the edge of the glass and knocked it off the commode before you had even had a chance to touch it. The leg with the butterfly on the foot broke off at the hip. Your fright was mixed with a thrill of triumph as you saw that the angelic child was totally hollow.

Wordlessly, your mother placed both pieces of the figurine, which were never to be reunited, back in their place, set the bell-jar over them forever, dragged you through the hall into the kitchen, bent down without letting you go, took a stick of birchwood from the basket by the stove, and hit you on the head with it. Dismayed by the blood which flowed down your face from the cut she had opened on your forehead, she cried out to you, oh my boy, my little boy, bandaged your head, washed your face, carried you into her bedroom, put you in her bed, covered you up, kissed you, and went out on tiptoe, closing the door softly behind her.

The world was instantly paralyzed. There was a picture on the wall of the Madonna ascending to heaven, surrounded by angels and towering clouds. No matter how hard you tried to imagine that her richly-creased robe was billowing in the wind, that the hand she stretched out toward heaven was sweeping in a great arc, that the cherubim were tumbling down from the cloud banks into immeasurable depths, everything remained as it was, with no meaning or motion. You wanted to cry out for your mother: you had already opened your mouth when you suddenly realized that you wouldn't be able to explain anything, that there was nothing that could be explained. You got up very quietly, slipped down the stairs to the kitchen door, and peeked through the keyhole, so that, if only for the wink of an eye, you could catch them motionless; through the keyhole you saw your mother, her shift unbuttoned, kneeling in front of Hermann, who was sitting with his legs spread and his head back, moaning softly to himself; you saw her head moving up and down slowly until suddenly, with a loud groan, he held it down with both hands and bent over her in spasms. They sat that way for a while. Then Hermann straightened up, your mother rose, and without covering her white flesh, walked over to the sink and vomited.

Even today I still close my eyes sometimes and imagine, as I used to do so often, a motionless calm; landscapes, streets and squares like picture postcards. And I control everything that happens. But outside my window, trees are rustling in the wind, like trees rustling in the wind.

# 15.

It's harder than one thinks to make friends on a sea
voyage. The close proximity of passengers strolling on
the deck, sitting in the salons, passing in the halls and
companionways, and sharing the ship's meals and parties, leads only, with the exception of a nod now and
then, a smile of recognition, and a few general remarks
about the constantly fine weather, to brief conversations about the increasingly shorter twilight as the ship
heads south, the proper sort of clothing to wear as the
wind turns cooler, the gleam of the sea under the full
moon, the splendor of the stars in the southern skies,
which nothing outshines, conversations which seldom
go beyond a mutual exchange of opinions on the subject
at hand. Of course I met a few people, for example the
woman who sits next to me at dinner, an elegant, older
woman with whom I stroll along the observation deck
each day in the late afternoon, when the sun decks have
emptied and a beautiful peace has descended which will
last until suppertime. She leans on my arm, taking tiny
steps which at first I found hard to match. She never
leaves her cabin without her umbrella, which I carry for
her, one with a massive silver handle, of a weight and
size suitable for a stately gentleman, which she uses as a
cane if she's walking alone. We talk in broken French

about the strange melancholy of sea voyages, the confusion of foreign coasts, the sudden feeling of happiness in port, the intense longing to live in unknown cities. She's traveled widely and tells of mountain landscapes, steppes and deserts, of being awakened by the cold in flapping tents, of the emotions she once felt while reading certain novels.

We are a much-noticed couple and fill the ship with rumors, Dona Brigitta, the frail widow of an immeasurably rich landowner from southern climes, and I, the young man of unknown origin, as we walk together each day at the same time, talking in a foreign language we command with equal uncertainty, so that the oddest misunderstandings arise. Once we were discussing the story of a young man from the previous century, who, having grown up under conditions of extreme poverty in the countryside, rises to the highest circles of society in the capital thanks to his charm and natural gifts only to fall into ruin through boundless ambition; we talked of how the story of his misery had touched our hearts and excited our sympathy, of the deep melancholy we both felt as we closed the book, which had stayed with us for weeks. Since we realized, as we spoke the hero's name aloud as if with one voice, that we had been talking about two different characters in two separate novels, we walked on a while in silence, totally bewildered by the similarity of our experiences based on memories of two different works, and finally joined the other passengers who lined the rail watching a brilliantly-lit ship passing in the opposite direction and talking animatedly about states of happiness: whether they would prefer to be with us or over on the other quickly-passing ship, now within shouting distance; for a moment or two a gentle breeze carried to us the sounds of a waltz. Opinions were divided on the matter. I sided with those who wanted to be on the other ship, but I didn't say so, because I couldn't have justified my wish; our ship too is illuminated far more brightly than necessary, the one dark midnight hour when only the navigation lights are on is meant solely to allow those passengers who are interested in astronomy to observe the stars more clearly, and waltzes are played daily. It seemed to me, as ridiculous as it may sound, that the one great love of my life was standing on the other ship, wrapped in a billowing coat, looking over at me, feeling as I did.

That evening, when the unknown ship had disappeared from sight, as if the ice had been broken in the course of the discussion, the passengers and those of the crew who were off-duty held a party. A mood of relaxation gradually set in that affected everyone on board, even me, reaching its highpoint after a Polonaise on deck when, overcome by the splendor of a gorgeous sunrise, people embraced, made friends, and exchanged kisses of brotherly and sisterly affection. After Dona Brigitta had taken her leave around midnight with a little smile (she couldn't allow herself to fall prey now to the memories of parties of her youth), I stood off to the side, without giving the impression that I wished to withdraw altogether.

As the noisy crowd began to break up, making dates to do things together in what remained of the journey, and repeating that they had never seen such a sunrise, with the sun so near you could almost touch it, I was repelled by the idea of returning to my windowless cabin and facing the prospect of a dream-laden daytime sleep; I turned instead to climb a narrow iron stairway I'd discovered on previous strolls around the upper decks, disregarding the signs closing off that area of the ship to passengers, which led to a spot I'd grown fond of due to its sweeping view. To my surprise I found the small platform, which was situated beneath the radio mast and lacked any protective railing, occupied by a figure in a billowing coat who was turned away from me, looking out to sea with a telescope. I was about to go back down when the figure turned. It was a man. He looked neither old nor young, and I had never seen him before among the ship's crew or the passengers. He motioned for me to come over and handed me the telescope. "Just look," he said, "how huge the sea is, how vast." And after a while, as I was searching the horizon for some point on which my eye could rest, he said, "and I can't even begin to imagine its depths."

## 16.

After they found him wandering about aimlessly in his
cloth coat, half-frozen in the deep snow of the slopes
above the tree-line, Jakob moved into the rambling
house without objection, because he liked the view of
the ordered landscape from the window of the room he
was given, and because he had been calmed by the
assurance that everything would remain unchanged for
as long as he liked. And when, at the end of the third
day, despite their black habits and high hoods, he finally
recognized by their laughter the three Sisters, who
showed him around the house and introduced him to
the residents—a recognition which was moving as well
for the three Brigittes after the long years of separation,
although they begged him earnestly not to reveal it,
fearing it might endanger their indissoluble bond—
Jakob no longer felt any inclination to be sad or ungrate-
ful. He unpacked the suitcases which had been sent after
him, placed his things in the wardrobe, arranged the
room, shoving the bed from the window to the wall and
the desk from the wall to the window after thinking it
over carefully, for although he would have liked to look
up at the stars on sleepless nights, he desired the view by
day even more, and hung above the bed the beautiful
picture he had drawn of his father, the three Brigittes,

and himself, standing side by side, holding hands and laughing, on the lookout point above the ravine.

Day after day, Jakob sat at the window and, since he lacked watercolors, although the Sisters promised to get them for him soon, described in his tiny handwriting the views of the jagged mountains, covered halfway to their summits with dark forests of oak, and above that by light green larch and silvery bushes, until, beyond the tree-line, only the rugged limestone cliffs arose; described the vine-covered hills in all shades of ocher, the orchards and vegetable fields of the valley in their various greens, and in clear weather the steeple-rich silhouette of the city on the broad alluvial plain in the distance; described by night in his notes the stars in the heavens with their constellations, and by day the blinding blue, which seemed to him bearable thanks to the deliberate limits set by the embrasure of his barred window, the three-fold staggering of the brick drain-work on the roof, and the tall hedgerow of yew trees that almost hid the high barbed-wire fence.

The months passed by in an unchanging daily routine.

When he had finally settled in he was given various small tasks in the kitchen and garden like the other residents, which he performed willingly but without joy, since they interrupted his more important work writing and drawing. Although it often seemed to him as if everything had been accurately described and sketched, each day delivered the views anew, needing to be newly grasped in words and images; the notes and sheets of paper piled up on his desk, and he went through them on the last day of each month, putting them in order and tying them up in monthly packets, identifying them with catchwords by month—Jaguar, Zebra, Mink, Mandrill—and piling them in the corner between the wardrobe and the door.

In the Sabretoothtiger month construction started outside his window on a new addition to the complex. First the fence was torn down, then the yew trees were felled, and while the site was being excavated, the foundation poured, and the complex series of walls for the cellar rooms erected, Jakob could look across the now bare slope of land to the highway at the foot of the mountain and watch the traffic, which until now he had only heard as a distant hum. He would watch the play of white, red, and yellow lights by night, and they seemed in all respects more deserving of description than the ordered movement of the stars. And so he began to note the endless traffic on the road in every detail. He counted the number of vehicles, arranged them in long lists by color, function, size, and direction—lists he could only analyze at night, since the rush hour began early in the morning, before the residents were even awakened by the staff.

In an effort not to fall behind in counting and analyzing, he began to neglect his duties in the house and garden, and finally to fail in them. He was in a race with the increasingly shorter days—spending every waking minute training his ear to differentiate and recognize the various motors' sounds, so as not be restricted to sight alone to completely understand the traffic, as his time would otherwise be reduced, rendering his efforts useless, to the late morning and early afternoon hours of fog-free winter days—when he was moved to another room in the back of the house which looked out upon the flat roofs of the business offices and the bordering wall of the hospital grounds, with the explanation that the construction noise might have a negative effect on his health.

All pleas and protests, all assurances, were offered in vain; it was several weeks before he was able to force them to return him to his original room, regardless of the effect, by refusing all food, a tactic he was able to carry through only because the Sisters visited him each night and strengthened his resolve.

Meanwhile the addition was rising higher, and Jakob, robbed of his view, spent his days watching the workers, bored at first and occasionally amused, but then with increasing interest as it gradually dawned on him that it was going to be impossible for them ever to complete the annex. For as the walls of the upper stories were being erected stone by stone, the lower floors were crumbling, water was rising imperceptibly but steadily in the basement, rotting the wood, peeling the plaster from the walls and cracking them, so that at last it was clear that the building could not be repaired as rapidly as it was disintegrating.

That didn't seem to bother the workers. In the evening, when their day's work was done, they waded in rubber boots or barefoot with rolled up trousers through water which was already nearly knee-deep and greeted with brief nods the manager who arrived each day at quitting time to view his project. Hands on hips, he discussed things with the builder, clapped him on the shoulder now and then, pointed here and there with a laugh, and seemed totally satisfied with the way things were going. When the construction workers had changed clothes and departed, he took a pair of rubber boots from the trunk of his car, removed his woven shoes, stepped into the boots, waded through clay-yellow water into the interior of the building, appeared at a window, stepped out cautiously onto a balcony, stood for a long time on the top story with the unrolled blueprint, comparing what he saw with the plans, measuring walls with long strides, openings with el-bow lengths, carefully noting the results of his measure-ments in a green book, even though he must have realized that they were only provisional, for within a few days the walls would be moved elsewhere, the openings filled in, and everything would have to be measured anew.

However, while no one could seriously believe that the project would be completed—neither the residents who gathered regularly at noon before the openings in the construction fence and discussed its progress, nor the workers who, when the water had risen so high that they could no longer wade through it, simply placed planks from the first story to earthen walls piled up for that purpose and now surrounding the whole of the construction area, nor the manager who arrived each evening, walked through the building, and as twilight began to fall, whistling through his teeth, lit the security lamps—not a single person involved with the project or affected by it shared Jakob's distress as it fell to ruin.

Jakob covered his window, slept by day, and wrote by night the unfinished story of a young man who never wanted to be anyone but the person he had been from the very beginning in his own mind.

## 17.

I would like to walk again, not like someone strolling through a sunny park, nor someone sauntering down the streets of a busy city, nor hiking on the open heath, nor walking for the sake of movement and sights, but walking to reach a goal at the end of a long journey across a mountain, along a river, upon a road which winds about for no apparent reason, through an open forest: not striking out blindly across the fields, nor sticking solely to marked paths, not in a rush, but still hurrying slightly, like someone who, as twilight falls, wants to reach his goal before darkness sets in totally, and alters his pace according to the distance he knows he still has to cover, risking a shortcut here and there, although there is in fact no reason, other than the lure of such comforts as a roof to sleep under, for shortening the route or saving time, since the thought of losing his way, as unlikely as that seems in this easily surveyed landscape, awakens an intense longing for a night beneath the trees, for the voices of strangers, for mysterious noises, for a fear which only the courage you've built up from reading a thousand tales can counter.

And I would like to carry a piece of luggage, not too heavy and not too light, slightly unwieldy, a medium-size suitcase containing underwear, a second pair of shoes, three shirts and a sweater, toothbrush and toothpaste, soap, a pocket-knife (with large and small blades, a can–opener, a corkscrew and saw, a nail file and a magnifying glass, scissors and tweezers), a raincoat, and a paperback edition of my favorite novel.

That's how I would like to walk, and on my walk I would think about all those things it's important for a person like me to think about.

# 18.

Good morning.

Good morning, Jakob! Come right on in. Sit down please. I'll be through in a minute. I'm just taking a quick run through the notes from our last conversation. We made a good deal of progress I thought. . . . Go ahead and light up. Did you sleep well?

Very well. A deep and dreamless sleep. The pills you gave me helped a lot.

A tried and true remedy. We've used it for years, no side effects and absolutely dependable.

Why did you take the chess set away from me?

We didn't exactly take it away. You should take a break. It'll do you good.

It was my only diversion, other than looking out the window at the construction site.

I know, but it's only a temporary measure. It wasn't good for you to spend half the night poring over the chessboard. I have nothing against your playing two or three games a day—perhaps with one of your colleagues. Old Mr. Vogel plays pretty well I think.

No, I prefer to play against myself.

But you get all upset.

No I don't, it calms me.

You may think so. We view it differently. You see, I

can't play chess. That is, I know how the pieces move of course, the bishops diagonally, the rooks straight ahead, the knights one forward one diagonal. But, I don't know, it all happens too slowly, and I lose the overall pattern. It makes me nervous, and I'm always infuriated when I lose a piece because of a careless move. At the same time I can imagine that it could be quite interesting, boring into the head of your opponent move by move. But when I try to imagine what it would be like playing against myself—it just doesn't work. One side would always know in advance what the other has in mind.

That's not always possible. You can learn to shield your thoughts, even from yourself. Or more accurately, a point is reached where you no longer take sides.

Oh, come on, you have to take sides! For instance: black moves his knight in order to threaten check on the next move. The king has to move out of check and the knight takes the rook. But since you're both black and white at the same time you spot the trap and can make a countermove with white. So you have to choose between black and white.

That's too simple—the way you're describing it. Those are premeditated moves. I wouldn't sacrifice a rook lightly. There's another principle involved. In a normal game of chess, when two people play against each other, there's a winner and a loser.

Or a draw—no decision.

A draw's out. A draw's no solution. It's defeat for both sides. In the past, when I played "correctly" as you would say, I preferred to lose rather than face a draw.

Whenever I could see that the game was going to end in a draw you could say I committed suicide.

Go on.

There's nothing more.

Keep on talking, you wanted to tell me why you prefer playing against yourself.

I didn't want to tell you anything. You asked me and I answered.

Yes, but you're the one who started talking about chess.

I want my chess set back.

I ordered the chess set taken from your room because I want you to sleep at night. When you sit in front of the chessboard half the night you're nervous and tense the next morning and can't concentrate on our conversations. And after all, we're not here to play chess.

I demand to know why I'm being held here against my will. I demand to be set free immediately.

Now don't start that again! We've discussed that time and again, and I really have to ask you to trust me. No one here wants to do anything to you. You've got to understand that—or simply believe it. And if you'll just help us a little we'll get where we're going in no time. It's not a matter of—Would you like some tea?

Yes, please.

Sugar?

Yes, thank you.

Lemon?

A few drops.

I think a few drops bring out the flavor too. People should really drink more tea. Coffee is just something you drink down, but you can really enjoy tea. I had a secretary once who was a real tea expert. She kept five or six kinds of tea in her desk, orange pekoe, Earl Grey, green tea—gods knows what all. It was a real ritual.

At home, when I was a child, we always had tea, but that was different. My grandmother collected lime blossoms, blackberry leaves, elderberries, apple peels, mint—mostly we had mint tea, but when we got sick, or had a cold—then we had blackberry tea—or was it lime blossom?—I don't know. The white linen sacks were always hanging in the attic, lettered with laundry ink. When we were children the attic was our favorite place to play. I still remember when the Americans came, our mother hid everything in the attic. The radio, the camera, the binoculars, and my soldiers. I had a huge number of soldiers. My favorite one was throwing a hand grenade. You could see how the hand grenade, a stick grenade, was about to fly through the air, and where it would land. A tiny toy explosion. It was too boring for the others, they were always boxing with Dad's boxing gloves, but I could lie stretched out for hours playing with the soldiers. The only thing was I didn't have enough Tommies and Frenchmen, but there were even black soldiers among them. I had tanks and trucks, too, and an open commander's Mercedes with Hitler inside; you could raise and lower his arm, and when you lowered the arm then he had both hands at his side and looked stiff and comical. One day my mother traded all my soldiers for a big bundle of earmuffs. She unraveled them and knitted us all trousers and sweaters. They scratched horribly. I still can't stand wool against my bare skin to this day. I can't wear wool

things. There's nothing worse than sweating in a tur tleneck sweater. The damp heat, the constriction. I' rather freeze. I can stand cold better than too much hea

Do you feel better in the winter than in summer?

How do you mean?

Oh, it's nothing important. It just seemed to me bit—well, let's say "unusual" that someone woul apparently prefer a cold dead season to the warmth c summer, since everyone loves the summer.

How can you say something like that? That's a fals generalization, Mr. Jakob. I'm not sure how I'd choos between a crisp cold winter day, with the air so clear hurts your lungs, and the sort of sticky sultry summe day that takes your breath away. Even at night there no relief. On days like those I often dream of going t Patagonia.

Patagonia?

The word itself is so beautiful. Patagonia. It sound like a make-believe country. A pure invention. A nc man's land with no one there, a land with no streets tramcars, or houses. Only an airplane flying over nov and then high up in the ice-blue sky. Silent, in tot silence. Only the wind, the sound of the wind on th bare cliffs and across the broad fields of pure snow. N trees and no blossoms, only the smell of snow from th Antarctic. A totally pure land, that's how I imagin Patagonia. Even as a child I was enchanted by it Patagonia appears in the first poem I ever wrote.

Can you still recite it?

Of course, after all it was my first poem. I was fiftee or sixteen years old when I wrote it. I knew then wha my life would be like. I was going to be an author, no,

great writer. I would write two books, both of them long true books about life, and then I would die, young and unknown. There would be no photographs of me and no definite dates; my date of birth, when I entered school, that kind of thing of course, but nothing else, not even my travels. No manuscripts and no literary estate, just those two books and perhaps a few drawings, landscapes, drawings of construction projects, seascapes, but in general no—

I don't want to interrupt, but I'd very much like to hear the poem about Patagonia.

It's not a poem about Patagonia. Patagonia is mentioned in it. It's a poem from what could be called my early period:

> they taught me
> simply everything about quartz
> Pythagoras
> Christianfürchtegottgellert
> Patagonia
> h two s o four
> they didn't tell me
> the rest

That's good.
You think so? I think it's pretty good too, somewhat arrogant perhaps, annoyingly precocious for a sixteen-year-old. How did it come up?

We were discussing your preference for coolness, coldness, and the attic where you played as a child. About the cold in the attic.

Yes. No matter how pleasant the attic was in winter,

on wintry days, I couldn't stand to be up there in the summer. The gluey heat, stuffy with swirling dust, you could hardly breathe. In the winter I always put on Dad's leather jacket. Too bad she cut off the epaulets in the end.

Epaulets?

Yes, the epaulets.

Was it the jacket of a uniform?

A black leather jacket with woven epaulets with two silver stars on them. Whoever wore the leather jacket was the colonel, the others were prisoners and had to do what the colonel said.

What did they have to do?

Whatever the colonel said!

Well, what?

Stand totally motionless, for example, until they couldn't stand up any longer, or let a handful of snow melt in their mouths.

Not very exciting games.

The others didn't find them much fun either, they preferred boxing.

And you, what did you do?

I played by myself.

But if the others wouldn't play with you, I mean, you couldn't be both the colonel and a prisoner at the same time.

Oh, that's simple enough. When I was wearing the black jacket I was the colonel, and when I took it off I was the prisoner. I put the jacket on and said: stand still and don't move. Then I took the jacket off and didn't move.

Tell me about the snow.

You had to put it in your mouth and let it melt. You had to put a packed snowball in your mouth, bite down on it, and wait until it had melted.

But didn't that just kill your teeth?

Of course it did, but that was the test!

Test? Test of what?

Or punishment.

Punishment for what?

For being a prisoner and having to do what the man in black said.

The game with the snow. You could only play that in winter. Where did you get the snow up in the attic?

That's easy. You think you can catch me lying, don't you? The snow stayed longest on the roof, all I had to do was open the attic window and there was soft white snow.

Of course, the snow was there. I wasn't trying to "catch you lying" as you say, that's nonsense. I just couldn't quite think for a moment where the snow was. So there was soft white snow on the roof.

The snow crusted over and didn't pack so well during a thaw of course, and further up, on the ridge of the roof behind the chimney the snow was dirty from the smoke. There were snow guards lining the roof. They kept the snow from sliding off. And there were two windows, one on each side of the grey slate gable roof, and there was a roof ladder too for the chimney sweep. I can't remember the exact number of rungs on it, but that surely isn't needed to judge my case!

No, please, there's no reason to get angry, Jakob. I'm not angry.

Or irritated.

I'm not irritated. You keep insinuating things—you're always making insinuations—

Please, I'm sorry, I'm—

always making insinuations that I'm—

not insinuating anything.

not telling you the truth.

I didn't mean to insinuate anything.

I demand an apology, Mr. Jakob!

I've already said I'm sorry.

In passing. That was only in passing, a turn of phrase, but not an apology.

Please accept my sincere apologies.

I accept your apology and request in the strongest possible terms that you stop doubting what I say. I have an excellent memory. It never fails me. I notice the smallest details. On our honeymoon I played a game of chess with my wife on the train from Verona to Florence. She opened with the queen's gambit, and I took immediate advantage of her foolhardiness, placing her constantly on the defensive. It was a won game from the first move. I was determined to take away any chance for development, to force her into merely reacting. I could have checkmated her on various occasions. I let her feel that. But instead I forced her into a position where she couldn't move. I moved my bishop from d2 to g5. Instead of withdrawing her king to e4 she lost her head completely and moved her pawn to b4. One of my pawns was on b3. I moved my knight from a6 to c5, covering the squares e6 and e4. G4 was covered by my pawn on f3, g6 was covered by my rook on h6. That was it. Do you know what it means for a chess player to

95

force his opponent into a position where he can't move? It's total victory, the total subjugation of the opponent, a humiliation of his mind.

And? How did your wife react?

She tried to knock the pieces over. But it was a traveling set. The figures had small pegs on the bottom that you stuck in holes in the squares. They stayed upright. And I left the whole game standing until we reached Florence. We didn't say a word to each other. We simply stared at the board the whole time. Is there any more tea?

Yes, help yourself.

Would you like some more?

No. No thank you.

Now, are you convinced? Do I have a good memory?

Yes, you've convinced me. You have a good memory.

Well, thank you!

Tell me about the epaulets.

Mother came up to the attic one day and asked "What are you up to now?" and I said, we're playing Colonel and the Prisoner. Then she took a pair of scissors and cut the epaulets off and took them away. And without the epaulets the game just didn't seem the same. She put them in the night stand. I found them once when I was sick. When we were sick we could sleep with Mother in her bed. They were in a blue velvet case, behind the rosary and the aspirin.

You often complain of headaches yourself.

If you mean by that, if you're trying to make some connection out of that, like I inherited that from my mother, I take after my father completely. Around the eyes, and the mouth. Even as a child, everyone said I took after my father, my dark hair, my mother was blond. I don't bear the slightest resemblance to my mother. My headaches are caused by completely different things. Bright light, oppressive weather, stuffy air, eyestrain, insomnia, very concrete things.

There's something I'd like to know. Why did you come back to the city?

My god, why'd I come back here? I wanted to see it again. I lived here. I know the city. What do I mean "know"? I lived here with my wife. After all those were important, decisive years in my life.

And happy years as well?

Happy years as well.

Was your trip planned or spontaneous?

What do you mean by planned—or spontaneous? I'd wanted to visit the city for some time. I was in the area, and so I decided to come, spontaneously, if you like.

How long did you live here?

Three years, almost four.

Up to when?

Until two years ago. But you know all that, why do you ask? I've told you all this before.

I'm sorry, I'd forgotten. Then you traveled a good deal.

My wife's income allowed me to travel a good deal.

Where?

Everywhere.

Even to Patagonia?

Even to Patagonia.

And?

And what?

Was it what you imagined it would be?

Patagonia is ugly, rocky, and barren. I should have stayed away.

I've read it rains a lot there.

Yes, it rains a lot.

Of course you visited your aunt when you returned?

My wife. No. I didn't visit her.

Yes, your wife. But that's strange. You hadn't seen her for two years.

We telephoned each other from time to time.

And then you're in the city and you don't even meet once—spontaneously.

She didn't want to. I told her I was coming, but she didn't want to see me, or speak to me.

And why was that?

I don't know.

Of course you know. Surely you must have asked?

No. My wife loves me and I love my wife. Without reservation. We both know that, and so we both respect what the other person wants and does.

But then your wife would have had to accept you as well, without reservation.

Respect.

I beg your pardon?

Respect, not accept. You don't understand and I don't want to explain it.

Explain what?

What you consider contradictions. You're trying to get me to contradict myself in a very stupid way, as if this were an interrogation in the movies. But there are no contradictions. Everything is as it is. Whether you like it or not.

My dear Jakob, I beg of you. Of course this isn't an interrogation. And if you've been given the impression that there's some, how should I put it, criminalistic aspect involved in our conversations—no, there really isn't.

I know. You want to help me, and if I tell you my life the way you want me to tell it, we'll soon reach our goal. What goal?

You're resisting again. Perhaps we should stop for today. We'll go on another time, when you feel better.

No, ask your questions. I feel fine. And I'm getting interested myself.

All right then. Why have you come back now, at just this time?

My travels were over. As I said, I was visiting in the area. It wasn't far out of the way. Otherwise it's pure chance.

I hope you'll forgive me, but I don't believe that. You chose what seems to be a very significant date for your visit. That couldn't have been a matter of pure chance.

The beginning of spring?

I have before me a report from the central hospital. On that day, the sixth of April of the previous year, you attempted suicide. You were admitted on the seventh. You remained under medical observation for four days, we can skip the medical details. You then spent four months under psychiatric care.

Enforced.

What do you mean enforced?

It's a complicated story. I don't see what difference it makes after all this time. It's totally unimportant.

I just want to discover the reason for it, the cause.

There was no reason, and there was no cause.

What did you do on that sixth of April?

I drank a little. Then I accidentally took too many pills.

Just try to remember. What sort of a day was April 6? Rainy? Sunny? Dull?

A thaw. Yes, there was a thaw. There were signs posted all over the city warning about roofslides. The sidewalks along the Burggasse were blocked off. A roofslide had killed an old lady.

So that morning you walked into town.

Rode in—on the tram.

Go on.

That's all. I rode the tram into the city and walked around a little.

Let's start over at the beginning. You got up.

Yes, of course.

You had breakfast.

First I shaved and took a shower.

What did you have for breakfast?

Oatmeal with milk, as always.

What did you wear that day?

I'm not sure anymore. Yes, I do know exactly. I was wearing a blue-and-white-striped shirt, a gray pullover, gray trousers, and gray woolen socks—and a pair of underwear. They were missing when they let me out of the hospital. And they'd forgotten to give me my shoes. I walked home through the city in my stocking feet.

After breakfast you rode into the city. Which line did you take?

Number 23. Listen, do you want me to tell you whether the streetcar was crowded or empty, what color eyes the conductor had, whether—

I want you to remember everything—try to remember every single detail.

There's no such thing as total recall. Haven't you ever lost a key you just opened the door with two minutes before, and then tried in vain to reconstruct those last two minutes?

Of course. That's why I'd like to try, with you, to discover what you did back then. As precisely as possible.

You leave your apartment and go across the street to buy something. You enter the shop and you no longer know what you wanted. Nothing happened as you were crossing the street to shock you, excite you, frighten you. Your mind is blank for a second, and you no longer know what you knew the second before.

But that's an entirely different matter.

I can only remember that day in general terms.

All right then, you were in the city, where?

In the inner city. And then I had a cup of coffee in a coffeehouse and watched the chess players. But I always did that.

Did you play too?

No. But of course you play along when you're watching a game. I don't think it was a very good game. Black gave up too quickly, tipped over his king and leaned back laughing in his chair, as if it didn't matter. But in fact his defeat was by no means inevitable. I left then. But that could have happened on any other day.

Go on.

A bus for Schwarzenberg was standing at the bus stop. So I went to Schwarzenberg.

Was there any particular reason for that?

No, the bus was standing there, I was bored, so I just took off for Schwarzenberg.

Had you been there before?

No, that's why I went. Because the view of the city from the mountain was supposed to be so beautiful.

Tell me a bit about the trip and the visit.

There's not much to tell. The bus was practically empty. Two women were sitting in front of me, wrapped in black scarves. They seemed to be asleep. The road rose steadily in sharp curves. Two men were sitting behind me talking in whispers across the aisle. They spoke softly and quickly in a dialect so that I could only understand fragments of their conversation. However, if I remember correctly, it had something to do with a case of jealousy and murder. Then I fell asleep. The driver woke me. The bus was already empty. It had rained. Then I went to the scenic point. It was a very poor view. I stuck a coin in the automatic binoculars. But I couldn't see anything, not even the church spires of the city. I got sick on the way back from the rocking of the bus and the bad air. When we got back to the city it was already dark.

What did you do then?

I went to a restaurant at the railway station and had a drink.

Do you remember what you drank?

Yes, of course. Red wine, that's what I always drank.

How much?

Three or four glasses.

And then?

Then I went to the movies. *Key Largo* with Humphrey Bogart and Edward G. Robinson.

You do have a good memory!

You can't forget that film.

Why not?

Because it's one of the few films where a story is really told to the end. It's definitely going to end in death and you can bet on Humphrey Bogart or Edward G. Robinson.

Who did you bet on? Who did you put your money on?

Oh, I don't mean really bet. It's clear who's going to survive. From the very beginning. All you can do is bet against yourself, because in your own case it's not at all clear. I mean if you're really involved in the film.

I don't understand.

Whether you would shoot. Or have the nerve not to, for example.

Did you shoot?

I don't recall. That changed from time to time. That's just it.

Did anything happen when you were in Schwarzenberg?

What would have happened? No, there was nothing. I already said, even the view—

Anything that might have shocked you?

No. Nothing. I told you.

Frightened you? Confused you?

I'm not saying anything more.

What was it about Schwarzenberg that made you go back there this year?

I haven't been there!

You were there!

I'm not saying anything more.

I know you were there. What happened in Schwarzenberg two years ago? Why did you go back there? Come on, tell the truth! I want to hear the truth! What happened? All right. When you came out of the movies that evening you went home and got drunk. Did that happen often? Did you get drunk often? And then you took sixty sleeping pills. Just like that. No reason. By accident. How did you manage that? You surely didn't swallow sixty pills one after the other! You dissolved them in water. In tea? A big glass filled with a milky fluid. It must have been a regular porridge. Did you picture yourself as a hero? No, you hurt yourself. Who did you want to punish? And when you had downed the stuff, how did you feel?

Stop it!

But you knew that your aunt would find you the next morning.

My wife.

Yes, pardon me, your wife. She would have knocked the next morning to bring you the newspaper or the mail, to wake you up.

Stop it!

All right what about it! The newspaper?

We didn't get the newspaper.

The mail!

I hadn't got any mail in a long time. Back then.

Ah yes, not back then. But you wanted to die back then. Why?

I had difficulties.

What sort of difficulties?

Personal difficulties.

Could you explain them please?

I've already said they were personal difficulties. I don't want to talk about them. Anyway they're not important.

Tell me.

I was fed up with everything, getting up in the morning, shaving, seeing myself in the mirror, my face, waiting for something that never came, the cold room, the dark hall. The path, always the same path from the room into the dark hall to the stairwell and back. Back and forth again and again to the drone of the loudspeaker. The streets. The words and images and all the stories. You can't imagine how much I hate this city and the snow. You can't imagine how much I hate the snow. The blinding white snow and the dirty black snow. Every morning hoping it would finally thaw. But new snow had fallen overnight, and everything was blinding white. It hurt my eyes, in spite of the snow goggles. The east wind carried dust with it that coated the snow black. The snow looked marbled—looked marbled. And the horrible yellow piss-holes in the snow and the blood.

Describe the images in your head. Tell me what you see. Tell me exactly what you see!

A white VW. A white VW is standing in a field, a snow-covered field. The door on the driver's side is open. The seat on the driver's side is tilted forward. A woman is sitting in the back seat. Her left leg is hanging out of the door, her right leg is lying slightly bent on the driver's seat, on the tilted back of the driver's seat. She's wearing boots that come up over her calves, just short of the knees. Her skirt is raised high above her waist. She's wearing dark stockings with a black border and garters. You can't see the upper part of her body and her head. She's probably asleep.

No, she's not asleep, she's dead.

She's still alive. I know.

Close your eyes again. Keep describing the images as precisely and accurately as you've just done. Come on now, it's very simple. They're all in your head after all. Describe her face.

I can't describe her face.

Clever, there isn't much left of her face all right. But the rest. Come on now!

Her jacket is unbuttoned.

And her blouse?

Her blouse is unbuttoned too.

Unbuttoned?

It's ripped open. There's a deep gash in her breast. Very deep.

The colors. Tell me about the colors.

The boots are black, so are the stockings. The skirt and jacket are red, dark red. The blouse is also black. The VW is white, a white convertible with a closed black roof. The snow-covered field is just above Schwarzenberg. It was April 6 of this year.

All right then. And now, let's have the whole story please.

I could tell you now that I was looking for her soul, but I can tell other stories as well, better ones perhaps. I know a lot of stories, and often enough I don't know whether they're my own stories or stories from books, or stories from movies, or TV stories. It doesn't really matter anyway, they all fit and they're all interchangeable. Sometimes the index finger of my right hand actually crooks as if to fire a pistol. I feel the point of contact, and my eyes are staring into the barrel, and I see the scene in my mind in the movie where Humphrey Bogart is looking into the barrel of a gun, and I have the same slight smile on my face. I'll tell you what fascinates me about playing chess against myself. It's the inevitable fact that I have to be the winner and the loser at the same time. And the snow. The snow isn't white like snow. The snow takes on any color I want it to.

# 19.

It's a strange thing about speech. Speaking is easy and difficult at the same time. It's easy when you're happy or very unhappy. In the case of both happiness and unhappiness, words to describe the state of happiness or unhappiness come easily. They seem to occur to the speaker automatically, since those who are happy or unhappy are not ashamed to use even the most shameless words, and since they say them without reflecting upon them, the shameless words seem quite true, so that the words used seem neither unspeakable nor inappropriate to the speaker or the listener. With regard to the question of words, then, unhappiness may be explained as a dark variant of happiness. As is the longing to express a beautiful pain.

But who has been happy for such long periods of time that he could completely forget how difficult it is to speak in all other circumstances?

How often one has words in one's head, important words that could express what one has always wanted to say, words which, at least in the moment they arise, one believes capable, if only they were to be spoken, of altering everything, the entire world, those who are speaking, and those who listen. But the words do not

emerge. They expire on the way from the depths of the head to the lips.

If the word-producing organs of our body function automatically in those moments when words seem to appear without our own volition, when we need do nothing, the production of words when we must find and choose them ourselves becomes a task which strains the apparatuses we do control. Many learned discussions on the opening and closing of the mouth, exhalation and inhalation, the role of the tongue in channeling the air stream, the vibrations of the vocal cords in producing vowel sounds, the nostrils as resonators for shifting consonants, the throat's broad latitude in forming both verbal and nonverbal gutturals, including the function of the uvula, have appeared in anatomical and poetological contexts. With regard to the fundamental question of the special role of the mouth beyond these elements: which parts of the body are related to the realm of the mouth by their influence upon the production of speech, only one study has, to my knowledge, offered meaningful results up to now, and tellingly, it is a poetic work. The author of this text includes in this category, to my mind inescapably, the earlobes and the fingers of both hands when inserted in the mouth. Unfortunately he only hints at the crucial connection between sexuality and the formation of speech when he equates speaking with shaving, an unjustified demand placed on men by nature, leaving them speechless before women. Meanwhile the characteristic phenomenon of the disappearance of words in the head has hardly been investigated. Studies of this unique and frighten-

ing state seek vague explanations in symptoms of deterioration of the brain as a result of age, alcoholism, overwork, or mental illness. The truth, however, as each person knows for himself, lies deeper. Thus if one seeks to discover the mystery of words in the mouth by opening it as wide as possible before a mirror, one is initially at a loss in looking at the mucilaginous opening which, behind the thick tongue, depressed with difficulty below the uvula retracting in spasms of nausea, stretches down darkly as a passage for nourishment and in no sense as a path for words. But if one leans one's head back, one realizes that it's better not to touch upon the mystery of the origin of words, a closed mystery which lies behind that beautifully corrugated vault, unless one seeks death simultaneously. One closes one's mouth and gazes involuntarily into one's own eyes.

## 20.

They granted my wish to visit the village of my birth without a judge's order, and I was allowed to travel without an escort. For that matter, I wouldn't have objected to an escort, for example one of my Brigittes. We could have shared our memories during the trip, guessed who among my many relatives might still be alive, whether they would recognize us first, or we them, and how and by what means. We would have fallen into our dialect, hesitantly at first, and then more and more fluently, recalling the strangest of words, expressing our fears of no longer finding such and such a person, laughing as we argued about the dates of certain events we remembered differently, calling upon our fellow travellers to confirm things that had supposedly happened at the same time, of varying importance. The trip would undoubtedly have been amusing. In retrospect it was, however, better to have traveled alone, since amusement was not the primary purpose of my journey. But I want to tell everything from the beginning.

The railway journey seemed much shorter to me than it was in actual hours. The early autumn landscape flew by beneath such bright sunshine that it was a pleasure to look out the window. Contrary to my habit of sitting so that I traveled facing forward, since I suffer from motion sickness, I had taken a seat facing the other way, because the sudden recognition of certain country scenes and city views seemed to me more surprising, and the chance to keep them in sight for some time afterward more exciting, then to see them approaching in the distance and then have them pass quickly by. I had to change trains several times. Thanks to planning my trip carefully, I made all my connections on time.

Having arrived in D., where a native first begins to hear the local dialect, I discovered that the railway line up the valley to my village had been discontinued. I regretted that deeply; I would have to leave unanswered the tense question of whether or not I would be overcome again by what I remembered as my happy feeling of anxious confusion as I used to ride along the little winding river through the fields and meadows to my village, wondering if along this short stretch where every railroad tie was familiar to me, my goal might not be receding from me at the exact speed with which I was approaching it.

The buses which now carried the workers from the villages of the neighboring vales to their workplaces in the main valley had altered their schedules to conform to business hours and ran only mornings and evenings. Since I had no desire to wait for several hours in the small unattractive industrial city, I took a taxi. The driver was a sullen and taciturn fellow. Although I had asked him to follow the road from village to village along the river, he took a new by-pass that was built

half-way up the southern slope of the valley. He justified his choice by claiming that the old road would not
take me to my goal. Since for the most part the new
highway ran through deep cuts and seldom offered
views of the valley, I asked the driver what had happened here that was new and of interest over the last few
years. Obviously disinclined to conversation, his re-
plies were brief and uninformative. I assumed that the
region had hardly changed at all. You can imagine my
surprise when, having rounded a lengthy curve to the
left, I suddenly saw a huge lake lying before me in the
harsh noon light. I must have cried out in shock,
because the driver pulled to a stop and asked if I was all
right. I said I'd never seen the lake before, even though
I'd grown up here. You haven't been here for years
then, the driver replied, driving slowly along the narrow road which led to the other side of the valley across
the long, sweeping curve of the dam, stopping at
appropriate places and pointing up and down the valley
to tell the story of its flooding. I listened and looked as
the realization set in that my home town no longer
existed, its inhabitants, as I learned, now lived in extensive newly-built settlements in the hills. The compensa-
tion for their property in the valley had made them
relatively well-to-do, and they had been able to increase
their wealth by providing all sorts of services for the
tourists who arrived in ever-increasing numbers to rest
and relax at the lake. Now coalesced into a large munici-
pality, the former villages no longer bore their old
names. The name of our village has been preserved
however. It now adorns a hotel with a restaurant and
bar widely-known in the area and popular with tourists,

built on the rocky island in the ravine. When I first told him my destination, the driver had naturally assumed that I meant this resort, for almost no one thinks of the village anymore when its name comes up.

The side of the mountain has been blasted out in such a way as to enlarge the small look-out point above the ravine into a parking lot. A cable-car connects the lot with the rocky island, which is covered by a large hotel and a variety of restaurants. The tables on the broad terrace were all taken. Several boats and yachts were moored at the long dock. And only their slight movement revealed that the water which now filled the ravine was still flowing.

I climbed through the forest with my luggage to the high meadows where now no cattle or sheep grazed, followed for a time a trail along the ridge marked for hikers, which I remembered as a cowpath with many branches, sat down on a bench carved out of half a log at a spot where signs had been placed with fancy lettering indicating it was a good location for photographs, and looked down on the lake. A white excursion steamer was heading across it for the island resort. Rowboats swayed in its wake. Sailors and windsurfers were profiting from a slight breeze. I had trouble identifying the mountains, hills, and forests on the other side of the lake. The sun was now low in the sky, leaving them in shadows which blurred their borders and made it difficult to judge distances. And so I was not able to find fixed points to help me determine the location of our village beneath the lake, let alone that of the house I was born in, except in the vaguest terms.

I closed my eyes and painted the summer lake white on white, as a winter scene. It must be wonderful to glide on whispering skates over an area of cleared ice the size of a soccer field, to a waltz in three-four time from distant loudspeakers, with arms outstretched, in great figure eights, crossing again and again above the site of all memories, an ice-skater unlike any skater before.

## 21.

Jakob looked down on the lake for a long time. He would have liked some reason to cry, but there was none. Nothing now lying beneath the water is worth mourning for, Moy said, stood up, pulled on his coat since it was turning cool, climbed down the mountain, and walked across the ice to the other side of the lake.

That's how it was. Or otherwise. I forget from day to day.

Journeys would explain things.

Journeys into the land of novels. Filled with people we know.

J. L. B.